BY TIFFANY REISZ
THE HEADMASTER
RITA AWARD NOMINEE

THRILLS! CHILLS!
NEW! 10TH ANNIVERSARY EDITION
I0716741

THE HEADMASTER

SHAFFER

The
Headmaster
Tiffany Reisz
Illustrated by Andrew Shaffer
8th Circle Press · Louisville, KY

I paint flowers so they will not die.

— FRIDA KAHLO

CHAPTER ONE

She'd never make it to Chicago alive.

Not unless she got some coffee. Stat.

Bone-weary from driving, Gwen pulled over and parked in front of a small diner at the edge of tiny Andover. She got out of her car and stretched her back. Her tail bone ached from the long drive. The thick September air felt heavy with the heat, the humidity wrapping around her body like a fur coat. When she inhaled, she caught the scent of the nearby Appalachian Mountains. Everything smelled so rich and alive—the dark soil, the beech and maple trees, the leaves taking their last breath of summer... So much life and beauty around her, and yet Gwen wasn't part of it.

She took her phone out of her messenger bag and snapped a quick picture of the mountains rising behind the little town.

Gwen stepped inside the diner and fifty years into the past. It looked like it had been plucked from 1960—or at least a sanitized version of 1960—with the chrome stools that sat belly-up to a white-and-red bar and the waitresses in their paper hats and white dresses. The Rolling Stones crooned "As Tears Go By" from a gleaming jukebox. She couldn't hear the song without thinking of her father singing it to her as a lullaby twenty years ago.

But her bladder demanded more attention than her memories. Inside the bathroom, Gwen noted the movie posters hanging in the stalls—*Bye Bye Birdie* and *Dr. No.* Conrad Birdie versus James Bond—she knew who she'd put her money on. Especially since, as an English teacher, she couldn't look at the title of *Bye Bye Birdie* without wanting to put a comma between the second "Bye" and the "Birdie." And maybe, just maybe, a hyphen between both "byes."

She washed her hands and glanced at herself in the mirror. She looked tired, her copper hair lying lank across her forehead. She found her favorite vintage newsboy cap in her purse, which she used to pull her bangs off her face. She wasn't sure if it improved her appearance, but at least it would keep her hair out of her coffee.

Gwen ordered two cups of coffee—one for here and one to go. As she sipped at the diner's counter, she mentally calculated how far she'd come and how much longer she had left.

That morning she'd left Savannah, Georgia at 10:00 a.m. She'd driven four-and-a-half hours—over three hundred miles. She'd probably sleep in Kentucky somewhere tonight, which would leave about four hundred miles to go to get to her friend Tisha's in Chicago tomorrow night. And then...what? Try to be the best houseguest ever while she job-hunted for a teaching position. Hopefully, she would get one quickly and wouldn't have to spend the next six months sleeping on Tisha's couch.

"Miss?" A man two stools away from her summoned the waitress. He looked to be in his mid-sixties.

"What can I get you, sir?" the waitress asked.

"Directions?"

"Where to?"

The man hesitated before answering. "You know old Marshal? It's been fifty years since I've been to the school."

The waitress smiled kindly at him. She patted the back of his weather-beaten hand.

"I'll draw you a map, sir. Easy to get lost out there." She took a pen from her pocket and doodled a map on the napkin while the older man watched and nodded. "And you'll turn here. Be careful because they took the old sign down."

"Thank you, miss," the man said, his voice wavering with emotion.

She handed him half a dozen napkins—white with red trim like the diner counters. "You take these with you. You might need them."

He nodded solemnly and put the napkins in his pocket.

Gwen watched the scene. Maybe the waitress had figured him for the sentimental type. Some people did get very nostalgic for their old schools, though Gwen doubted it was the school so much they missed nearly as much as their lost youth and innocence.

"I'll draw you a map, sir. Easy to get lost out there."

Still, the man had piqued her curiosity. Gwen took her phone out and searched for "Marshal School" and "Andover, North Carolina." Nothing came up.

"Don't even bother," the waitress said to her. Her nametag read LILY. "We're in a dead zone out here—no 4G, no 5G, no nothing. You gotta drive five miles north just to pick up any internet."

"It's okay. I was trying to look up the Marshal School."

"The Marshal School's about ten miles from here, right on the edge of town. Boarding school. Progressive, the school says. Ask me, I say it's weird."

"Weird how?"

"Rich parents send their kids off to a school where they can't even use their phones?"

"I don't know. As addicted as kids are to their phones, it sort of makes sense. You know if they're hiring?"

"They're usually hiring. Goes year-round so teachers get burned out there pretty fast. You a teacher?"

"I am," Gwen said. "I was a T.A. at Savannah State. I didn't get any classes for this fall."

"You want to go teach some crazy high school students, Marshal's the place for you."

"I'll take any job that'll have me," Gwen said.

Lily tilted her head and gave her a sympathetic look.

"Divorced?" she asked.

Gwen laughed. "No. Just dumped. And even then, I can't blame him. My boyfriend moved to Africa to teach ESL. Something on his bucket list, he said. I couldn't afford the apartment by myself and with no classes to teach..."

"Been there," Lily said. "Divorced and jobless. Ended

up here." She waved around the diner. "Nice place. But if they don't put some modern music on the jukebox soon, I'm liable to take a golf club to it. Would a little Adele kill them?"

Right now, Janis Joplin was singing her heart out about freedom, about how it was a synonym for "nothing left to lose." The English teacher in Gwen doubted she'd find that phrase in a thesaurus next to "freedom," but she was inclined to agree with Janis.

"I feel like I'm in a time machine," Gwen said. "James Bond watched me pee."

"What a pervert," the waitress said, smiling. "And this whole damn town is stuck in 1964, but that's how it is sometimes. Can't go back. Can't go on. Might as well stay where the good Lord put you."

Gwen wasn't sure she agreed with that, but she thanked the waitress and quickly finished her coffee. She paid her bill and followed the older man out of the diner.

"Sir?" she asked, and the man turned around. "Can I look at that map of yours for just a second?"

"Of course, young lady." He gave her the napkin map, and she took a picture of it with her cell phone.

"Thank you. Why are you headed to Marshal?" she asked him when she returned the map.

"Went there a long time ago. Graduated in 1963, so I'm a lucky one, I suppose. Thought I'd visit some old ghosts, that's all." He shoved the map into his suit pocket. "You be safe out there."

"Thank you, I will. You too." She smiled at him, but he didn't seem willing or able to smile back.

As she walked back to her car, Gwen considered

whether or not she wanted to drive out to Marshal and see if they were hiring. The waitress Lily seemed to think they were. It wouldn't hurt to ask, would it? Although she didn't look much like a teacher right now in her jeans and boots. Well, if the school was as weird and progressive as Lily said it was, maybe they'd appreciate her outfit. At best, she might end up with a teaching job and not have to drive to Chicago. At worst, nothing would come of it, and she'd keep driving.

She returned to her car and ensured all the boxes she'd stuffed into the backseat and passenger seat were still secure. She'd packed everything she owned into her Camry yesterday. She was twenty-five years old, newly single, with no job, both parents dead and gone. So why not go begging for a job at a boarding school in the middle of nowhere on a random Friday afternoon?

Janis Joplin would ask her what she had to lose. The answer? Nothing.

Gwen pulled up the hand-drawn map on her phone and headed out, carefully following the instructions as she drove down the twisting mountain roads. The map marked the entrance at a certain spot on Lexington Lane, but it was so overgrown with ivy that Gwen missed the turn the first time she passed it. Going five miles an hour, she finally spied an old stone post. She turned and drove two miles through a canopy of trees casting shadows and sunlight onto the road.

But this couldn't be it, right? Who would tuck a school this far from civilization? She would've turned the car around, except the road was too narrow. She had no choice but to keep going until she could find a spot to turn around. Then, just ahead, she saw what appeared to be the end of the road.

"Beautiful…" Gwen breathed as the school slowly came into view. Where she'd expected a gleaming state-of-the-art industrial new school, all glass and steel, she found an enormous four or five-story red brick school-house, like something out of a Dickens novel, enclosed by tall moss-covered stone walls.

She followed the road to the cobblestone drive that led through an opening in the walls. In iron lettering, a sign welcomed her to THE WILLIAM MARSHAL ACADEMY. She stared at the sign for a long time. Something kept her from driving forward, and something else kept her from going back.

Fear. Fear held her pinned in place as if an invisible hand from high above pushed a fingertip to the top of her car. She imagined if she hit the accelerator, the wheels would do nothing but spin impotently in the dirt.

She recognized this fear because she'd felt it before. It wasn't anxiety as the doctors defined it. It wasn't a panic attack, either. It was change. All her life, when she would stand hovering on the threshold of a new experience, she froze in place, trembling. Her first day of college, her first date with Cary, her first night with Cary, her first job teaching… Every time she stepped onto a new path, she'd faced the terror of the first step. Snap out of it, Gwen ordered herself. It was just another school, and maybe they'd hire her, and maybe they wouldn't.

"Beautiful..." Gwen breathed as the school slowly came into view.

Yet she might as well have been walking a tightrope across a canyon with no net. The terrible unknown lay beyond the gates, beckoning her in and warning her away, and she didn't know which message she was supposed to believe.

She took her foot off the brake and set it gently against the accelerator.

Then, out of the corner of her eye, she saw something. A flash of brown fur and black eyes at her passenger window. With a scream, Gwen slammed the accelerator, and the car shot forward like a bullet. The wheels caught gravel, and the car slid sideways, and in a second that lasted for eternity, metal twisted, blood dripped, and the scent of smoke filled her nostrils. The last thing she saw was the deer that had done the deed staring at her with blank, bright eyes that did and yet did not see her. And with one mighty leap, it was gone as quickly as it had appeared.

Gone. And so was Gwen.

CHAPTER TWO

Gwen woke up in fits and starts. She'd open her eyes only to feel the weight of consciousness pressing back down on her. *Back to sleep*, it seemed to say in a male voice, imperious and irrefutable. She did as she was told. She could do nothing else.

When she woke up again, she didn't try to open her eyes. Instead, she used her other senses to gauge the damage. She sensed her body was whole and that no tubes or needles ran in or out of any veins. The pain was localized to the side of her head. Nothing else hurt. She wondered if she had a concussion. Did concussions cause hallucinations? She heard improbable, dreamlike voices all around her.

First, she heard a man's voice. British? Yes, his accent was definitely that of an Englishman, proper and educated.

But other voices answered his—younger ones, eager ones, scared but delighted for some reason.

How did she get here? a boy asked.

I wish I knew, the Englishman replied.

Will she live? came another boy's voice.

Can we keep her? asked another.

And another said, *Don't let her leave.*

Go back to class, you vagrants, the man said, and no one dared defy him. *Let the poor girl rest.*

She wanted to tell this pompous man who'd invaded her fever dreams that she was a grown woman and not a poor girl. And it was pretty rude of him to call the boys in her dream "vagrants," but when she tried to speak, to say to him, *I may be poor, but I am twenty-five,* nothing came out but soft, incoherent mumbling.

Gwen lapsed into a deep sleep again.

———

HOURS OR DAYS LATER, she blinked her eyes open. She was finally awake. Carefully, she moved her head left and right, then her arms and legs. She seemed to be okay. No broken bones. A few cuts and bruises.

What happened? She vaguely recalled a deer and broken glass. And then...nothing. Unconsciousness.

But where was she? That was the real mystery.

She looked around and found that she lay in a king or queen-sized bed with white sheets, a deep green-and-gold brocade blanket, and an ornately carved walnut headboard. On the nightstand sat a Tiffany lamp and a black rotary phone.

Something about the dark colors, the heavy furnishings, and the scent of the sheets—sandalwood, maybe?—

convinced her she was in the bedroom of a much older man.

With a groan of pain, Gwen forced herself to sit up. Her head swam as soon as she was vertical, but it quickly passed. Gwen put her feet onto the rug and slowly stood up. How long had she been in this strange man's bed? Why had she been brought here instead of taken to a hospital? Behind the closed bedroom door hung a polished oval mirror. She looked like herself. She had some bruising around her left cheek, and a white bandage had been applied to her temple. When she ran a hand through her hair, slivers of glass came out.

She was dressed but not in her regular clothes. She had on a man's white shirt, a buttery soft brushed cotton. Someone had taken her clothes and shoes off of her. At least she still had her underwear on, but where were her shoes and all of her other things?

Carefully she eased the door open and called out a shaky, "Hello?"

No answer.

She retreated into the bedroom again. A door on the opposite side of the bed led to a wood-paneled bathroom, as masculine as the bedroom she'd found herself in. Whoever lived here must have been an old-fashioned sort —instead of an electric razor, a straight razor in a case sat on the bathroom counter next to a white-bristled shaving brush. A leather strop, the sort her grandfather had used to sharpen his kitchen knives, hung from a hook on the wall. The bathroom smelled of leather, soap, and other pleasant male scents—bergamot, citrus, cedar.

Gwen turned on the tap and drank cold water out of

her hands. How long had she been unconscious? She was dehydrated but not enough to be sick from it. Her mouth felt like sand and her head throbbed, but she sensed she would be fine. The bathtub, an old porcelain monster, beckoned to her. She'd love to wash the glass from her hair. She knew she should look for the owner of this bedroom, this bathroom, this...wherever she was, but she'd been in a car accident and had a head injury. She had an excuse to do whatever she wanted, and what she wanted was to get clean.

She filled the bath with warm water, stripped naked, and sank into the heat. Sighing with pleasure, she submerged herself fully in the water, letting it soak her bloodied hair and her bruised skin. When she raised her head out of the water, she felt healed. The wound on her temple was still there. No miracle had occurred, but she did feel better than she would have dreamed she would from something as simple as bathing in warm water.

As blissful as she felt in the bath, she didn't dally. When she was sure she'd washed all the shards of glass from her hair, she stood up, pulled a fresh white towel around her, and stepped onto the floor. She'd gotten water and a little blood on the shirt she'd been sleeping in. She dreaded putting it back on. Then she spied a pale blue striped-silk bathrobe hanging on the back of the bathroom door. It looked like something Sherlock Holmes would wear. She knew she was being more than a little presumptuous stealing the bathrobe of whoever lived here, but she'd blame her bad behavior on her accident.

She slipped the robe on. She swam in the thing. Had to belong to the man who lived here in this...house?

Apartment? And the man must have been very tall, broad-shouldered and handsome.

Handsome?

Gwen froze, her hands on the silk cord she'd just knotted around her waist. A man stood in the doorway to the bedroom. From the expression on his face, she could see he was shocked to see her on her feet. Or maybe he was shocked to see her wet and wearing only his bathrobe. She didn't know the exact reason for his shock, but he was shocked, and the feeling was mutual. She'd been right. He was tall. He was broad-shouldered. He had black hair peppered with grey and wore silver-rimmed eyeglasses on his strong-jawed and handsome face. He looked no more than forty but every day of forty.

"I'm sorry," she said when she'd recovered her powers of speech. He seemed like the sort of man one apologized to for the crime of daring to be undistinguished in his utterly distinguished presence.

"Might I ask what you're sorry for?" the man said. "That way, I know what trespass I'm forgiving."

"Um...I guess this is your bathrobe?"

"Dressing gown."

"I don't know where my other clothes are," she continued. "I can take this off if you—"

He held up his hand.

"Wear it," he said. "Please."

"Are you sure?"

"Quite sure. You took a bath, yes?"

"Yes."

"And you've had water, I assume?"

Odd question. Or maybe not. Maybe she'd been

passed out long enough he was concerned she'd gotten dehydrated.

"I drank some water. I wouldn't say no to another glass?"

His face was unreadable and his silence made no sense to her. She got the weird feeling he was almost disappointed. Or maybe not disappointed. Sad?

"Of course. Of course, you did. And yes, you can have a glass of water." He stood up even straighter, and his frame filled the doorway to his bedroom. They stood a moment in silence, studying each other. She felt acutely aware of her wet and naked body under the dressing gown, and although the man's eyes never left her face, she sensed he was acutely aware of it as well.

"Do you have a name?" he finally asked.

"Gwen. Gwendolyn Ashby. And you are?"

"Edwin Yorke. I'm headmaster here."

"Headmaster? Am I at the school? The Marshal School?" Her memories of her conversation at the diner came back to her.

"The William Marshal Academy," he corrected. "And yes, you are."

"Oh, well, that's good then. I was coming here. Someone in town said you all might be hiring?" She made the sentence a question, hoping the answer was yes.

"Are you a teacher?"

"English and literature," she said. "I'm an amateur grammarian and a professional reader." Gwen smiled. He didn't. She soldiered on. "I was on my way here to see if there was a job opening. Actually, I was going to Chicago, but thought I'd try my luck here—"

"You crashed your car into the side of my school."

Gwen winced. "Sorry about that. I was trying to avoid a deer. I hope no one was hurt."

"Someone was hurt."

"Oh, no. Who? It wasn't a student, was it?"

"*You* were hurt."

"Oh, yes," she said, her panic immediately subsiding. "Is there much damage?"

"Only to you and your car. I don't think you'll be driving it for a while."

"I should call a tow truck, I guess." She didn't have much money, and a tow truck would take half her gas budget for her trip to Chicago. And God only knew how much repairs would cost.

"We'll worry about all that later," he said as if her problems were his problems. "You should eat and rest. I'll have the boys bring your things up."

"The boys? You have children?"

"I have sixty children."

Her eyes went wide.

"Students," he said with a tight smile. "Here at the Academy."

"Small school. All boys?"

"All boys. You are, in fact, the only female on campus right now."

"And here I am in your bathrobe. I mean, dressing gown."

He was quiet a moment, looking at her like he hadn't seen a woman in years. Maybe he hadn't?

"You're staring at me," he said.

"You're also staring at me. But I have a head injury. What's your excuse?"

She couldn't quite believe she'd said that out loud. It was the head injury talking, she told herself.

He raised his hand. "Stay," he ordered.

She stayed.

He left her alone in his bedroom again, and she sat on the bed. Looking down, she saw the robe had opened enough that the headmaster of Marshal had gotten more than a glimpse of her cleavage. The only woman on campus? She didn't know how to feel about that. The headmaster—Edwin Yorke—had been nothing but a gentleman to the near-naked, obviously concussed woman who'd stolen his bathrobe. And he was handsome. And English. And tall. And did she mention handsome? Maybe she should stop focusing on how attractive he was and get back to focusing on how screwed she was right now.

She ran her fingers through her wet hair to tame it. In the other room, she heard voices, whispers, and laughter. The laughter sounded young, much younger than the headmaster. Then the door reverberated with the sounds of seemingly a dozen hands knocking all at once.

"Who's there?" she called out.

"Laird," a teenage boy's voice answered. "I'm a very nice person. I promise."

"If you weren't, would you admit it?" she asked.

"No, I'd probably lie and tell you I was nice," he admitted.

"Are you lying?" she asked.

"Headmaster Yorke is standing right here. He'll make sure I'm nice. Or he'll kill me."

"Then you should probably come in before he kills you," Gwen called out. "I can't have your life on my conscience."

He opened the door with one hand, and with the other hand, he covered his eyes.

"I have your things from your car," Laird said, his hand still shielding his eyes.

"No, you don't," she said. "You have nothing with you."

"I couldn't carry the bags, open the door, and cover my eyes all at the same time."

Gwen smiled. Not that Laird could see that smile with his hand covering his eyes. He looked about seventeen or eighteen with dark red hair and a sweet face—what she could see of it.

"If you can handle seeing a woman in a bathrobe, you can uncover your eyes," she said. "If you can't, just back away slowly, and I'll get my own things."

"I can handle it," he said and lowered his hand. He stared at her through narrowed eyes. "Are you married?"

"Excuse me?"

"I'm not asking for me," he said.

"No, I'm not married."

"Good. You're hired," Laird said. At that, an arm reached into the room, clamped down on Laird's shoulder, and bodily dragged him back out the door.

In his place, her suitcase appeared.

"It was nice to meet you," Laird shouted from behind the door. "Please stay forever."

"Nice to meet you, too, Laird." She walked over to her suitcase and bent over to pick it up. It was then she realized Headmaster Yorke was standing outside the bedroom door and had likely seen straight down the bathrobe. She flushed crimson, but he merely looked past her.

"Dinner is in half an hour," he said, his voice cold and strained. He handed her a glass of water. "You'll dine here in my quarters. I won't subject you to any further scrutiny by students. Yet."

"I'll get dressed," she said.

"That would be an *excellent* idea."

She dressed in the best clothes she owned—a pencil skirt and white blouse—and in half an hour, she went looking for the headmaster, the dining room, or both. She found an elegant mahogany dining table laden with food (whitefish in sauce, celery hearts, chilled honeydew melon) and wine (red and blush). It was a feast for a king, but the king never showed. When the headmaster said she'd be dining in his quarters, she'd assumed it would be with him. She didn't want to think about why his absence disappointed her. She wanted to talk about a job—that was why. Of course.

Disappointed or not, she still ate every bite on her plate and then some. When was the last time she'd eaten so well? Living on a T.A.'s income had meant living on student rations. Now sated, Gwen left the table and wandered around the headmaster's quarters.

From the window by the dining room, she saw she was on a high floor of a building. Maybe the brick building she'd seen while driving up to the school? She must have been five stories up. No elevator on the floor, from her cursory inspection. How had she gotten here? Someone must have carried her up the stairs. A student? The headmaster himself?

Gwen walked from window to window as she tried to get her bearings. From her high vantage point, she could see the square stone wall surrounding the grounds. Outside the wall, the forest loomed dark and wild. Inside the wall, there were manicured lawns, walking paths, and several other buildings. Gwen was clearly in the tallest of the buildings. To the left and right of her, she saw two smaller buildings of wood and stone. Another building peeked out from the back. Cobblestone walkways connected all the buildings. A turret of sorts rose from each corner of the wall. Turrets? Stone walls? Was this a Southern high school or an Ivy League university? Or a dream?

Wherever she was, it was beautiful. Breathtakingly, heart-stoppingly, daydream-inducingly beautiful. Already, she sensed herself falling under the spell of the school. She could hear the heels of her shoes clicking on the cobblestones, her books tucked under her arm. She saw herself sitting on the stone bench under the overhanging oak tree, grading papers. She could imagine herself here, teaching, happy.

She'd never let herself hope or dream that she'd be happy—really happy, not just not miserable—someday. Maybe when she was a kid, she had assumed happiness had been possible for the likes of her. But that was before her mother had died of cancer when she was little and her father of a heart attack when Gwen was a freshman in college. She'd found stability, if not grand passion, with

Cary. But then she'd lost him, too, when he'd gone to follow his bliss. Safety and stability—that was happiness to her.

But...

What if she did get a job as a teacher here? What if she could stroll those paths, sit under that tree, teach a student like Laird, and take orders from someone like Headmaster Yorke? Then...maybe...just maybe...she could have safety, stability, *and* happiness.

Or maybe that was just another daydream?

Gwen left the headmaster's quarters and found the steps that led downstairs. She wanted to see her car and assess the damage. But once she reached the second-floor landing, she heard the sound of voices in a faraway room. Talking and laughter. She followed it to the source past empty classrooms. It was evening. Of course, no one was in class. But something was happening behind the door at the end of the hall.

Gwen opened the door and stepped into a magic forest.

CHAPTER THREE

The magic forest was made out of paper-mâché and Christmas lights. Gwen felt a hand on her elbow. Headmaster Yorke pulled her by his side and raised a finger to his lips. He nodded, and she looked ahead at the play in progress.

A boy with dark hair stood in the center of the paper forest and looked around as if lost.

"Do I entice you?" the boy asked. "Do I speak you fair? Or, rather, do I not in plainest truth, tell you I do not, nor I cannot, love you?"

He delivered his lines with conviction but also a slight stammer.

"Christopher Hayes." Headmaster Yorke whispered the name into her ear, and Gwen shivered at the feel of his breath on her neck. "He could barely get a full sentence out when he started here at Marshal."

"And now he's acting in plays?" she whispered back.

Gwen was incredulous. Not only because Christopher

was acting in a school play with a stammer, but also because none of the students were teasing him when his voice stalled. Not even one laugh. Astonishing.

Again the headmaster nodded, but this time she could see the gleam of pride in his eyes and the smile that threatened to take over the severe lines of his face.

She turned her attention back to the play rehearsal.

The redhead called Laird was also starring it seemed. He wore a tablecloth like a skirt over his school uniform. The boys in the audience whistled and he rolled his eyes. There. That was better. Much more normal boy behavior. She'd been worried the headmaster beat the boys into submission.

"Shut it," Laird yelled at the crowd. "I'm trying to Shakespeare over here, all right?"

That only incited more whistling and laughter.

"Now I forgot my lines. Line?" Laird called out.

Whoever was supposed to be prompting him had clearly fallen down on the job. With a sigh, Headmaster Yorke picked up the playbook and started leafing through the pages.

"And even for that do I love you the more," Gwen called out. "I am your spaniel. And, Demetrius, the more you beat me, I will fawn on you."

The room fell silent. Every pair of eyes had turned to study her.

"Use me but as your spaniel," Laird continued. He looked into Christopher's eyes and spoke again. "Spurn me. Strike me. Neglect me. Lose me. Only give me leave, unworthy as I am, to follow you."

Gwen stepped back into the shadows and the play

continued. Side-by-side with the headmaster, she watched until the intermission at the end of the second act. As the boys in their costumes and uniforms rearranged the scenery, Headmaster Yorke led her out into the hallway.

"You have *A Midsummer Night's Dream* memorized?" he asked her.

"Yes, and *Hamlet, Richard III, Henry V*, and most of the comedies—the good ones."

"You're not an actress, are you?"

She laughed at the disdain in his voice. Why were the English so good at disdain?

"Just a mere teacher," she said. "A teacher with a really good memory. I always have my students act Shakespeare out. You can't truly understand a play until you see it performed. Shakespeare especially. I had no idea he was funny until my junior year of high school when they took us to see *A Comedy of Errors*."

"Tell me—" he began, but a familiar redhead opened the door and stuck his head into the hall and interrupted.

"Did you hire her yet?" Laird asked. "We need a new English teacher."

Headmaster Yorke turned and glared at Laird. Laird winced and made a hasty retreat.

"As I was saying," the headmaster continued. "What are your qualifications as—"

Now Christopher's dark head appeared in the doorway.

"Are you the new English teacher?" Christopher asked without stammering.

"She is," Laird said, standing next to him in the doorway. "Her name is Gwen Ashby."

"Hello, Miss Ashby," Christopher said. "You're not married, are you?"

Headmaster Yorke answered the question for her by putting his hand on Christopher's head and pushing him back through the doorway. Laird's head popped through the door.

"Have you ever read *Ivanhoe*?" Laird asked.

"I'm afraid not."

"Oh, thank God," Laird sighed with obvious profound relief. He pointed his thumb at the headmaster. "He's made us read it six times."

The headmaster glared at Laird so hard that Laird seemed to shrink back into himself.

"No more *Ivanhoe*, please," he mouthed as he disappeared back through the door.

"You have very interesting students," Gwen said. "I like them."

"I don't."

"Liar," came Laird's voice from behind the door.

Behind his glasses, Headmaster Yorke looked up at the ceiling. "Is it still illegal to kill students in America?" he asked.

"I'm afraid so, yes," Gwen said, suppressing a laugh.

"I'll simply have to risk it. Come with me to my office, Miss Ashby."

"Yes, I will. Thanks for asking."

He arched his eyebrow at her.

"I was pretending you asked me, instead of ordering me," she said.

"But you are coming to my office."

"Yes, since you asked so nicely."

He looked at her, turned on his heel, and stalked down the hall.

She knew he expected her to follow him immediately, so she paused, counted to three, and then followed him. She wasn't a well-trained dog, after all.

The sun was sinking but hadn't set quite yet, and long slants of golden light poured in through the windows in the school building and set everything alight. The floors, walls, and windows looked like they were on fire with so much sunlight, and ahead of her, the headmaster cast a long shadow that she stepped into as he led her up the winding stairs.

They came to a room that was likely Headmaster Yorke's office. He had a grand desk, a large leather chair, and windows behind him that would allow him to look down onto his school. And books, so many books in his office. Shelf after shelf of leather-bound volumes. No paperbacks. Not a one. This man took his library seriously.

He gestured to a chair in front of his desk, and she sat down. He took a seat in his high-back leather chair, steepled his hands in front of his chest and stared at her.

"You won't like it here," he said. "I strongly encourage you to leave if you can."

"Is this how you start all job interviews?"

"Yes."

"Is this like that scene in *Fight Club* where you tell me to leave and I get the job only if I stay?"

"The scene in what?"

"*Fight Club*? The movie? Ever seen it?"

"I'm a busy man, Miss Ashby. I don't waste time on popular entertainment."

"I'll adjust my references accordingly then. Look, Mr. Yorke, I—"

He raised his hand to silence her.

"I realize you're seeking employment, and I respect that," he said. "But it would require an enormous sacrifice from you to become a teacher at this school. I left my home country years ago and have never returned. The students are here year-round. We work year-round. We teach year-round. We have everything we need here at the school, and we rarely leave the grounds. You would be required to commit yourself to this school as we have. Whatever life you have outside the walls of the school, you would have to give it up to remain here."

"I appreciate your concern, but it's safe to say I have no life outside the walls of this school. Having a life inside the walls of this school would be one more life than I have right now."

"I find it hard to believe that a lovely young woman such as yourself has no life."

"I don't have any family anymore except for grand-parents I don't see very often. Mom died when I was little. I had to switch colleges my freshman year after my father passed, and I lost touch with all my friends in the process. I had a boyfriend. He moved to Africa. So when I tell you my entire life is in that car I wrecked trying to not kill a deer? I mean it." She paused a moment. "Also, you think I'm lovely?"

He ignored the question. "My condolences on the loss of your parents."

"Thank you." She swallowed a sudden lump in her throat.

"You look very young, Miss Ashby."

"I'm about to turn twenty-six. Definitely old enough to teach high school students."

"Even students such as mine? The boys here are precocious and highly intelligent. They require constant intellectual stimulation to keep their minds occupied. One student, bored by his classes, turned the courtyard statue of our founder, Sir William Marshal, into a jet-propulsion experiment."

"I didn't see any statues in the courtyard."

"That's because the experiment succeeded."

"Oh. Wow." She almost said something about the movie *Real Genius* and how it could have been worse—the headmaster could have ended up with a building full of popcorn or an indoor ice rink. But she kept that reference to herself.

"Indeed. It would be unfair of me to ask such a young and...lively woman to give up her life to teach here. I'm afraid you'll simply have to be on your way as soon as you feel up to it."

Gwen might have agreed with him. She might have left. She might have packed things up and packed it in and packed off to Chicago like she'd originally planned... but something stopped her. What was it? The headmaster had called her "lovely," which she liked. She liked it very much. She felt herself drawn to him more than any man she'd ever met. But there was more to it, though she couldn't say why. It felt like she was meant to be here.

"I think I'd like to stay if you'll have me."

The headmaster raised his eyebrow and Gwen blushed.

"Have me as a teacher here," she continued. "I've never met students who were that excited about Shakespeare. Please let me teach them."

The headmaster stared at her. He seemed to be weighing something in his mind. Her merits? Her virtues? The pros and cons?

Or maybe he was just imagining throwing her down on his massive desk and having his way with her? Probably not.

"You may stay," he said, and Gwen opened her mouth to thank him. He raised his hand to silence her again. "For a one-week trial period. It will take a few days for you to get things sorted out, and I wouldn't want you to leave until we were sure you're completely healed anyway."

"One week. I can handle that."

"There's something you must understand about this school before stepping into a classroom. The William Marshal Academy is not a normal school. It's not an average school. It's not typical by any means. Other schools say they want to train students and make them leaders. A leader is nothing. A leader is simply one who leads, and a bad leader can lead an army into Hell. I want these boys to be heroic, brave, and wise. Like our namesake Sir William Marshal, the greatest knight in history."

"I think that's a very noble purpose," she said, admiring Headmaster Yorke's vision for the school and his passion for improving not only the minds but also the character of his students. "And I promise I'll do what I can to help."

"I'll simply be relieved if a week passes and you've not done them irreparable harm," he said and pointed at his desk. "This is my office. Do not bother me when I'm working in it."

"Can I bother you when you're not working in it?"

"No." He stood up and snapped his fingers. Obediently she rose to her feet. Hero or leader or simply handsome headmaster, she was ready and willing to follow him anywhere. Or at least out the door. "The other teachers have their offices in this hallway, as well. Mr. Price teaches math and science. Mr. Reynolds teaches history and philosophy. I've taken over the teaching of literature as Miss Muir has left us."

"Where did Miss Muir go?"

A shadow of something crossed his eyes. "I can't say."

"Can't say or won't say?"

"Both and neither. Miss Muir is none of your concern. Your work will be your only concern. This is the office you may use during the week you're here."

He took a key ring out and opened the door. She loved the quaintness of the keys. These weren't cut at Home Depot on a machine. They looked like keys to a castle gate. He opened the door and she peeked into the office. Gauzy white curtains graced the windows. Instead of Headmaster Yorke's carved wooden monstrosity of a desk, this little office boasted a petite writing desk with a feather pen and inkwell.

"No computers?" she asked.

"Computers?" Headmaster Yorke said with abject derision as if she'd asked where the dungeons were instead of the computer lab. "I don't know what sort of school you think this is, but we have nothing to do with computers here. They can learn that in university if they wish." He said the word *computers* like he was pronouncing a word in a foreign language.

"Interesting," Gwen said. "That waitress in town said Marshal didn't let students have phones. No computers either?"

"The students here use books. Books and pens and paper. Handwriting is taught here. The art of letter writing. I will not allow these boys to leave this school without knowing how to write a proper thank-you note. When you grade their work, you will grade their thoughts as well as their presentation. Form and content go hand-in-hand."

"So I have to grade their handwriting, you mean."

"Precisely."

"I can do that."

"You *will* do that," Headmaster Yorke said as he closed and locked her new office door. "And more. I expect you to draw up a lesson plan for the week that is challenging enough to keep their interest. What was the last novel you taught?"

"*Great Expectations,*" she said.

He nodded. "Perfect. The library should have enough copies on hand. I'll have them boxed and waiting for you there tomorrow. You have two days to rest and prepare for class on Monday."

"We won't get very far in a week," she said. Her

college students at Savannah State had taken twice that long just to read it, and then another week to compose their papers. "Perhaps there's a shorter book—"

"The boys are fast readers," he said, cutting her off. "Also, before I forget to mention it—since Miss Muir has left us, there have been no women on campus. You'll likely feel unwelcome here and lonely."

Gwen looked up at him. She had to crane her neck a bit. "You're very handsome and charming when you're being overbearing and disdainful."

Behind his glasses, Headmaster Yorke's eyes widened in momentary surprise. "Then I shall endeavor to be less overbearing and disdainful in the future."

"Pity," she said.

"As you will be the sole female resident at William Marshal, you'll have your own cottage." He stood by a window and pointed at a small Tudor home that sat back far behind the main building. Gwen inhaled and covered her mouth with her hand.

"What is it?" Headmaster Yorke asked, sounding concerned.

"Nothing..." Gwen shook her head. "It's just so pretty. I get to stay there?"

"Yes, for one week while you're teaching."

"Thank you," she said in a small voice.

"It's only a house," he said, seemingly surprised by her enthusiasm.

"I'm sort of homeless right now. I planned on sleeping in my car tonight. I can't believe I'll be staying in that house."

Headmaster Yorke looked at her and, for the first time,

he seemed to see her. She wondered what he thought as he looked at her. His eyes were not unkind, only curious.

"You were planning to sleep in your car? That's not at all safe for a young woman. I would never allow that if I were your husband or father."

"No husband. No father. I'm on my own."

"Not anymore. You're here at Marshal now and under my protection as long as you remain here. And you will not be sleeping in your car. That's madness."

"I was moving to Chicago," she said. "I have my whole life in the car, and I didn't want anyone breaking into it."

"Better possessions stolen than your life endangered."

"You're very chivalrous."

"I'm merely sane, Miss Ashby. Will you be missed in Chicago?"

"No. I only know one person there, and she was going to let me crash on her couch. So this..." She pointed at the cottage. "Well, thank you. I appreciate it. More than I can say."

"You're welcome, Miss Ashby," he said, and for once all the glaring ceased. When he was glaring, he looked very handsome. When he wasn't glaring...well, he probably should start glaring again or Gwen was going to have even more wildly inappropriate thoughts about her new boss, like the one involving his enormous desk. "But remember, this is only for one week. Don't get comfortable."

"I'll do my best," she said, knowing she would likely never be comfortable in this man's presence.

"The male instructors are in that cottage," Headmaster Yorke continued, pointing another out. "If you require assistance during your time here, Mr. Price or Mr. Reynolds will help you. The dormitories are there and there," he said, pointing at the two smaller buildings that flanked the main building. "The fifteen- and sixteen-year-olds are in Pembroke. The seventeen- and eighteen-year-olds are in Newbury. My quarters are on the top floor of this building—Hawkwood. The library is on the first floor. Classrooms on the second and third floors. Offices here on the fourth floor."

"So you get the entire top floor? Nice."

"I am the headmaster. I need to be able to survey the entire school at all times—day or night. The safety of my students is my duty and my responsibility, a duty and responsibility I take very seriously."

"I believe that," she said when she saw the steadfast determination in his eyes. He was gazing upon the school grounds like a king on horseback surveying his realm. "I'll go get settled into the cottage. I need to call my friend in Chicago first. Thank you. Thank you for everything."

Gwen turned and headed for the stairs.

"Miss Ashby," Headmaster Yorke called out after her. She paused at the top of the stairwell.

"Yes, sir?"

"Understand this, Miss Ashby—these boys are my students. I guide them, guard them... I won't see them hurt or harmed or disappointed. The world is full of people simply waiting for the chance to disillusion them. But while they are under this roof, they are safe, they are encouraged, and they are cared for and guarded. And they are *educated*."

He put the greatest emphasis on the word educated.

"I'll take good care of them, I promise. And as for 'educated,' I can promise they'll be smarter by next Friday. Now if you'll excuse me, I need to unpack."

"Yes, speaking of that…" Headmaster Yorke strode toward her and stopped only inches from her. She ignored a thrill of excitement at his closeness. The English department at her school was easily ninety percent women. The few men she knew were all married and older. None of them had Headmaster Yorke's presence. *Stop it, Gwen. No crushing on the boss.*

"Speaking of packing bags?" she asked.

"Yes. Your wardrobe."

"My wardrobe? What about it?" she asked.

"I would appreciate it if you dressed…"

Gwen looked down at her clothes. Her blouse was a V-neck. Maybe a bit too much v for the headmaster's liking?

"How should I dress?"

"Conservatively."

"How conservative? My skirts go to my knees."

"I would prefer floor-length, but I suppose that's impractical."

"I'm afraid I didn't pack my parka and nun's habit."

"This is a school of teenage boys. And a young woman as lovely as yourself might prove to be a distraction."

Gwen's hands tingled. "That's the second time you've said I was lovely."

"I've seen worse."

"I appreciate the miserable attempt at a compliment, Headmaster. And maybe instead of expecting me to dress like a nun, we should train the boys to respect women no matter how they are dressed?"

"You have met teenage boys before, have you not?"

"Fine," she said flatly. "I'll try to find some burlap bags."

She started down the stairs.

"Miss Ashby?"

"Yes, sir?" She paused on the landing.

"If for whatever you reason you decide not to stay here with us, please allow me to apologize for my ill temper. I was not expecting you. Or anyone. Since Miss Muir left, we've had no ladies here. I believe I've forgotten how to behave around one."

"Thank you, Headmaster. I appreciate that. I didn't take anything you said personally. Except for the part where you said you found me lovely. I promise you won't regret giving me this chance."

"I might not regret it. But perhaps you will."

She thought he was making a joke, but no amusement shown in his eyes or on his face. She smiled at him anyway.

Smiling still, she left the main building and headed for her car. She took another look around. Beautiful...so beautiful was William Marshal Academy that she wanted to take a picture of everything she saw—the turrets, the little Tudor cottages, the winding cobblestone paths, the stained glass windows. She could scarcely believe it was real.

She pulled her phone out of her bag and found that she had no bars. Not a huge surprise. The waitress had warned her the area was a cell phone dead zone. Gwen walked down the path but picked up no signal at all. She'd try contacting Tisha again tomorrow. She headed back to Hawkwood Hall to retrieve her things from the headmaster's quarters. In a row of windows on the second floor, she saw several huddled teenage boys staring at her, a question in their eyes.

"He's letting me stay!" she called out to them.

They cheered the news, and Gwen could only shake her head in wonder. In what world were teenage boys excited to get a new English teacher? Was this North Carolina or Heaven? Whatever it was, it was her home now for one week.

One week. And then maybe...just maybe...forever.

CHAPTER FOUR

Gwen insisted on carrying her own suitcase from Hawkwood to the cottage Headmaster Yorke had said would be hers. The house was even more charming close up than it was from a distance. She couldn't believe she would get to live here full-time if she got the job.

At the arched front door, so quaint it hurt, she slipped the key into the lock and turned it. Trembling from excitement, she stepped into an elegantly appointed foyer. On her right, she saw the parlor with antique patterned sofas and carved wooden chairs. On her left, she spied a smaller room with a writing desk. She had her own office here, too? Wonderful. She wouldn't even have to use the one at the school. Then again...the headmaster had warned her not to get comfortable. Did he really have no intention of keeping her on at all after a week? She knew she'd pass a background check, and as long as she had a place to live and three meals a day, she could live on a small salary. All she could do was her best and keep her fingers crossed that the headmaster liked what he saw. She certainly did.

Gwen walked slowly through the downstairs room. Something about the house seemed so familiar to her. She had a sense, not of *déjà vu*, which she knew meant "already seen," but something more like a dream she couldn't quite remember. What did they call that? *Déjà reve*—"already dreamed." That was it. She felt like she'd dreamed this place before and was now seeing it in the light of day.

Impossible, of course. Maybe it was just the lighting. This cottage had the same sort of lighting as her grand-parents' house, the same sort of table lamps and flickering yellow bulbs. A moth danced around the ceiling light. She let it be. No moth had ever hurt her feelings. She welcomed its small, fluttering company.

So quiet...so peaceful...so serene. She heard no traffic from the highway this far back in the woods. Silence reigned here, an almost unearthly silence. She closed her eyes and could almost hear her heartbeat, her breathing. No TVs on. No video games, cell phones, or music blaring through speakers. After living next door to college students for years, Gwen considered the quiet a taste of paradise.

But it wasn't completely silent, as every single floorboard in the old cottage creaked when Gwen carried her suitcase through the hallway and up the stairs. She counted fourteen steps on her way up. She could walk from one end of her old apartment to the other in fourteen steps. Now she had an entire cottage to herself. Two whole stories. A grand parlor. An office. A kitchen and dining room. Heaven on earth.

She laughed when she opened the door to the bathroom and saw the antique claw-foot bathtub. She would live in that bathtub. It could easily fit two people. Two people? Not a terrible idea. She allowed herself a single second to imagine herself and the handsome headmaster in that bathtub...

She pushed the thought out of her head. No. No. Absolutely not, Gwen, she scolded herself. He might be tall and wickedly handsome with a posh British accent, but she knew better than to get involved with a coworker, let alone a boss. There were rules against that. Good rules. Smart rules. Sensible rules. She would follow them.

You know...unless he didn't want to.

She blamed that thought on the head injury.

Gwen opened the door to the master bedroom.

"Wow," she said aloud. She'd never seen a prettier bedroom in her life. The bed itself wasn't much larger than a double, but it had a blue-and-gold embroidered headboard that arched four feet over the top of the pillows. The bed linens were white, lush, and soft. She sat on the edge of the bed and sank deep into the sheets.

On the nightstand sat an oil lamp. A real live oil lamp. Gwen hadn't seen an actual oil lamp in years. Her grandparents had a couple as backups for when a storm knocked out the electricity. Gwen opened a drawer and found a book of matches. She struck a match, lifted the glass chimney, and lit the lamp.

Gwen opened a drawer and found a book of matches. She struck a match, lifted the glass chimney, and lit the lamp.

Soft firelight danced across the room. This was what the world once looked like. No electric lights. No LEDs or fluorescents. There was a time when people had made it through the night only by the stars, the moon, and fire.

She put the matches back and noticed a book tucked far back in the drawer. She pulled it out. A Bible. Not the typical hotel room Bible, however. This one sported a genuine leather cover—black and supple. She flipped open the front page and saw a name written inside it: *This Holy Bible belongs to Rosemary Leigh Muir.*

So this Bible belonged to her predecessor then? Headmaster Yorke had been annoyingly cryptic about what had happened to the woman who'd once held the position of English literature teacher at Marshal.

Perhaps she'd quit the job after an argument. Perhaps she and Headmaster Yorke had disagreed over the curriculum. Perhaps she'd grown tired of the year-round schedule? But she was gone now, and Gwen was here instead.

Not for the first time, Gwen considered the reality that she was the one and only woman at William Marshal Academy. Would this cause any sort of problem?

Surely not. The boys were all far too young for them to see her as anything but an old lady. Besides, she'd always preferred older men. Cary had been almost thirty when they'd started dating shortly after she'd graduated college. Headmaster Yorke appeared about forty—the perfect age in her estimation. Old enough to have achieved maturity and wisdom. Young enough to still be... Gwen paused and searched for the right word.

Virile. Virile was the right word. He might be the

glasses-wearing headmaster of a boarding school, but his deep voice, broad shoulders, and overwhelming presence made him the picture of masculine virility. Working for him was going to be a little harrowing. Especially if he called her "lovely" one more time. Although she did find it funny that he managed to make "lovely" sound like a personal failing on her part.

Well, she wasn't doing it on purpose.

Smiling to herself, Gwen put the Bible back into the drawer before she accidentally happened upon that verse that said something about not lusting after your new boss. She should try to find out what happened to Miss Muir so she could mail it back to her. Although Gwen wasn't particularly religious, she respected the beliefs of others. It might be a family heirloom, too. According to the copyright date on the inside, the book had been printed in 1920. A hundred-year-old Bible was certainly worth something to someone if only for sentimental value.

She laid the mystery of Miss Muir aside while she unpacked her bags. As soon as she was settled in, Gwen got to work jotting down notes for next week's lectures and class discussions.

Boys loved Dickens. Especially *Great Expectations.* Young Pip aids a convict, meets a crazy woman, falls in love with cold-hearted Estella, and learns valuable life lessons about who is and who is not his friend. They were going to love crazy Mrs. Havisham's decaying wedding dress and the moldy, rat-eaten wedding cake. It was a wonderfully Gothic tale, practically a horror novel.

Monday, she'd introduce them to the life and works of

Charles Dickens and give them an introduction to *Great Expectations*. Tuesday, they'd talk about the first three chapters. And so on. She had it all planned out. A perfect week. And if the kids clicked with her, Headmaster Yorke would see the wisdom in hiring her permanently.

She was already beginning to map out the rest of the school year in her head. Last semester, she'd taken a seminar on the Brontës, so their books were fresh in her mind. Great novels, although possibly a bit too feminine for a class of nothing but boys. No romances for a while— not until they learned to trust her judgment. Dickens first, and then onto the Brontës and Jane Austen.

She could see herself here a long time, teaching... walking...talking with students...reading...in meetings with the headmaster...long meetings...dinner meetings... *breakfast meetings...*

A loud bang startled Gwen from her wandering thoughts. Was that her front door? She'd been so lost in the quiet of the cottage, she'd almost started to believe everyone had gone to bed. She dashed down the stairs, glanced through the window, and saw two boys standing outside on her porch. She opened the door.

"Boys...hello there," she said. "Christopher, was it? And Laird?"

"That's us," Laird said. "We came to say hello and see if you needed anything."

"We're the welcoming committee," Christopher said. "So...welcome."

"A committee of only two?" she teased.

"More boys wanted to join the welcoming committee," Christopher explained. "But they weren't welcome."

Gwen laughed and the boys smirked and nodded at one another.

"Well then, I'm glad you two took the time out of your not welcoming people onto the welcoming committee to welcome me to Marshal. This is a beautiful school."

"Thank you," Laird said with a bow. "I built it all by myself."

"You did a spectacular job. Can I have a tour?"

"You can, but that's not our area. We'll have to send you the touring committee for that."

"Who's on the touring committee?"

"Everyone who's not welcome on the welcoming committee," Christopher said with only the slightest trace of his stammer.

"So what does the welcoming committee do since they don't give tours?" she asked, crossing her arms and leaning on the door frame. The boys looked at each other again.

"I don't know." Christopher ran his fingers through his hair. Cute kid. He had a young John Lennon look about him with his shaggy haircut, suit, and skinny tie. "We formed the committee about five minutes before we knocked on your door."

"We should have planned this better," Laird said. "Sorry, we haven't welcomed anyone before."

"You didn't welcome Miss Muir when she got here?"

"She was here before us," Christopher said. "And she wasn't all that welcome."

"You didn't like her?" Gwen asked, curious about her predecessor.

"She didn't like us very much," Laird said and

shrugged. "Her loss. And our gain. We have you, and you like us."

"Very much," she said. "And I like the school, too. So far."

"Tell her the thing." Christopher prodded Laird in the arm.

"The thing?" Laird asked. "Oh, the school thing. Sure. I can do that."

Laird paused and cleared his throat. Christopher hit him in the chest.

"The William Marshal Academy," Laird began his speech, sounding like a well-rehearsed tour guide, "was founded in 1893 by General John Foley, gentleman hero of the Union Army."

"The school," Christopher continued, "was established to take the best young men of America and train them in the ways of academic scholarship and ethical learning."

"The school motto is *Fortius quam fraternitas nullum est vinculum*," Laird said.

"There is no stronger bond than brotherhood," Christopher translated for her.

"That's very impressive," Gwen said, applauding.

"You should also know that Thursday night is roast beef night, so try to have something to do on Thursday night," Laird said.

"Not good?" she asked.

Christopher mimed slicing his hand across his throat.

"Good advice," she said. "I'll be sure to take it. Anything else I need to know about the school?"

"Headmaster Yorke isn't married," Christopher said.

Gwen pursed her lips at him.

"What?" he asked. "I thought that was important information."

"The headmaster's personal life is none of my concern," Gwen said. "Has he ever been married?"

Laird raised his eyebrow at her.

"I said it's not my concern," Gwen said. "I didn't say I didn't want to know."

"She has a point," Christopher said.

"So?" Gwen asked.

"He *was* married," Laird said, nodding. He leaned in closer. "I heard he's...you know."

"What?" she whispered.

Christopher looked around as if checking for spies.

"The D word," Christopher said in an even lower whisper.

"Deranged?" Gwen asked. "Demonic? Dying?"

"Divorced," Laird said, his voice strangely grave.

"Oh." Gwen shrugged, amused by how shocked the boys were over a divorce. "It happens."

"Does it?" Christopher asked. "My parents said they'd rather die than ever get divorced."

"I'd rather die than ever get married," Laird said.

"You and me both," Christopher said. They shook hands. "But the headmaster should get married."

"Does he have any children?" Gwen asked.

"Other than us?" Laird said. "No. Unless he got wild in the war, and there's an illegitimate Edwin Junior frolicking across Europe right now. But I can't really picture that."

"Edwin Junior would never frolic," Christopher said. "Not if he takes after his pops."

"Here's the thing, Miss Ashby. The man needs a wife," Laird agreed. "And you're the top prospect."

"I am?"

"Also the only prospect," Christopher said.

Laird nodded. "He needs someone younger than him so she can keep up with him. I caught him reading Shakespeare's First Folio in the northwest turret last week."

"That's bad?" Gwen asked.

"He was correcting it."

"Cry for help?" Gwen said.

"A loud cry," Christopher said. "So he needs someone young and pretty. Mainly because we prefer that. But she has to be smart, too. He'd go bonkers unless he had a smart wife. He needs someone to lecture."

"Pontificate at even," Laird said.

"Someone who isn't us," Christopher said.

"Boys? Can I ask you a question?" Gwen asked.

"Anything, Miss Ashby."

"Did you cajole Headmaster Yorke into hiring a new literature teacher because you need a new English literature teacher? Or are you all trying to play matchmaker for the headmaster?"

Christopher looked at Laird. Laird looked at Christopher. They both looked at her. This was becoming a habit of theirs.

"Yes."

CHAPTER FIVE

After breakfast on Saturday, Gwen went to the library in Hawkwood Hall to pick up the books the headmaster had said would be waiting for her. Several students were reading leather-bound hardcover books and writing diligently while hunched over in the library study carrels.

She scanned the shelves. The library was as well-stocked as any school library she'd seen. They had all the great classics here...all the great classics written before 1900, that was. Nothing from the twentieth century, as far as she could tell.

The only other adult in the library was a wizened gentleman with a cane—Mr. Reynolds, the school's history teacher. He was seated behind a large wooden desk. Must have drawn library duty for the day. She introduced herself and, out of curiosity, asked where the Hemingway, Faulkner, and Fitzgerald books were.

"Headmaster Yorke doesn't approve of modern literature," he said. Then, in a whisper, added, "We hide them in the back."

"Modern literature? *Hemingway?*" Gwen laughed. "He's hardly Franzen or Foer."

"Who?" Mr. Reynolds asked. He adjusted his eyeglasses. They had thick lenses and black frames like the ones her grandfather had worn while in the army. Mr. Reynolds had a hawk nose and a willowy rasp to his voice. He could have been anywhere between sixty and a hundred years old. Gwen guessed closer to the century mark.

"There was supposed to be a box waiting for me," she said. "*Great Expectations?*"

"Of course," said Mr. Reynolds, reaching below the desk. "They're somewhere around here...oh, here we are."

He hoisted a cardboard box onto the desk and slid it to her. Gwen opened the top flap and yes, there were close to three dozen musty hardcover copies of *Great Expectations*.

"We have every book you'll ever need," Mr. Reynolds said with a wink behind his Coke-bottle lenses. "Just ask."

"Every book?" she said. "Sounds like Heaven."

"It's a library," he said. "To me it's the same thing."

That was the moment Gwen knew she had to stay at this school for the rest of her life. These were her people.

Gwen signed a slip of paper for her books, and Mr. Reynolds peeled off the carbon copy and gave it to her. Carbon copies? Hilarious. One more bit of antiquity that had survived and thrived at Marshal. This school was weird, but it was a good kind of weird. Her kind of weird.

Headmaster Yorke seemed determined to give his students a classical—or at least Victorian—education.

There wasn't a piece of modern technology on campus. No cell phones, no laptops, no Kindles or iPads. Electrical lights were as close as it came.

There were some students out on the lawn playing a stripped-down version of baseball. No catcher. Just a pitcher, a batter, and a few boys scattered around the bases. She sat down on the steps and watched them. Their laughter and playful insults kept her entertained for an hour.

———

THAT EVENING, she had dinner in the dining hall. She sat with the math and science teacher, Mr. Price, who told her all about his years at Marshal. He'd been here twenty years, he said. Loved every single day, too.

"And Headmaster Yorke," she asked, trying to keep her voice neutral. "How long has he been here?"

"Ten years," Mr. Price said. "We worried that the new headmaster was too much of an English gentleman when he came. Didn't know if he'd melt in the heat."

Gwen glanced across the room where Headmaster Yorke, who clearly hadn't melted, stood in quiet conversation with another student. The student had a notebook in hand, and he and Headmaster Yorke appeared to be going over a bit of homework.

"He surprised us all," Mr. Price said. "Took to this place like a duck to water. Never met a more dedicated headmaster in my life. Good man."

"Good man when he's not threatening to murder the students, right?" she teased.

Mr. Price chuckled. "My dear, that man would die for these boys and they know it. I can't tell who's more loyal to whom—the headmaster to the students, or the students to the headmaster."

Gwen watched Headmaster Yorke and the student. She thought about the word Mr. Price had used. *Loyal.* Definitely a strange word to describe the relationship between high school students and their principal. Had she felt any loyalty to her teachers? Not that she recalled. Affection? Yes. But loyalty? It was a military term almost. Patriots were loyal. Soldiers were loyal. Did the students consider themselves squires, young knights-in-training loyal to King Edwin of Yorke? The headmaster did have a certain regal bearing to him. Head high, strong jaw, perfect posture, and broad shoulders that belonged on a soldier far more than on a teacher. And such penetrating eyes. Every few moments, he glanced her way, and she felt his gaze on her as much as she saw it.

What was he trying to see when he looked at her? She didn't know, but she did love the way he looked at her. She wondered if he was lonely here at the school with all this responsibility and no one to share it with. Maybe she could ease his burdens a bit by taking over the literature classes. Maybe she could ease his burdens a few other ways...

No pretending otherwise. Gwen knew when she was in the throes of a full-blown crush. Even if she hadn't found him so attractive, he was still fascinating. What brought a man all the way from England to become head-master of a boarding school in the middle of nowhere? And was he divorced, or were Laird and Christopher just guessing? If he was divorced, what happened? Did his wife come with him to America and hate it here? Did he leave her? Did she leave him? Gwen could certainly sympathize with being left behind. They should talk about it, get to know each other. If he was half as good and noble as Mr. Price said, she could only benefit from befriending him. If he was a king and the students his knights, surely he could use a lady in his court.

Either that was the head injury or the crush talking. Gwen was quickly figuring out that a crush and a head injury were basically the same thing.

———

AFTER DINNER, Gwen returned to her cottage and started to reread *Great Expectations* for at least the fourth time in her life. She hadn't liked the book when she first read it during her high school days. But a professor in college had opened the book up to her and showed her its secrets. Now she loved it and hoped the boys would, too.

So engrossed was she in her reading that when a knock sounded on the door, she nearly jumped out of her skin once more.

"Stop doing that, Gwen," she chided herself. She was going to have to get used to how quiet it was out here in the foothills of the mountains. Breathing deeply to calm her racing heart, she went to the door and opened it, expecting to find Laird and Christopher standing on her porch again. But no, it was Headmaster Yorke. So much for calming her down. Her heart raced faster in his presence. She needed to have a long talk with her heart about that bad habit.

"Why on earth did you do that?" Headmaster Yorke demanded. Even at eight in the evening on a Saturday, he still had on his three-piece suit.

"Do what?" she asked.

"Open the door."

"You knocked."

"Yes, but you didn't enquire first who was outside your door, did you? I could have been a murderer."

Gwen narrowed her eyes at him. "If there was a murderer on the other side of the door, do you think he would volunteer that information to me?"

"You should still ask before you open the door."

"Oh, fine," she said and slammed the door in his face.

The knock sounded again.

"Who is it?" she asked, singing the words in a playful mocking trill.

"Jack the Ripper," came the reply.

She opened the door.

"Good Lord, young lady, you are trying to get murdered," he said with utter disappointment written all over his face. Utter disappointment looked so handsome on his face that she resolved to disappoint him again.

"I think Jack the Ripper is fascinating," she said. "I'd love to talk to him."

"Before or after he murders you?"

"Either. Would you like to come in, Headmaster?"

"That would be highly inappropriate."

"Mr. Price was in here earlier today helping me with

the stove. Mr. Reynolds and I are having tea together tomorrow."

"Mr. Price and Mr. Reynolds are both widowed and elderly."

"Whereas you are young, handsome, and single, and your students are trying to find you a wife," Gwen said.

"None of that is even remotely true."

"I beg to differ," Gwen said.

He stood up straighter. "I'm old, ugly, and have been married."

"You don't look a day over forty, you're very attractive, and the boys volunteered the information you are divorced. That makes you single now, whether you like it or not."

Headmaster Yorke took a deep, steadying breath. "Miss Ashby."

"You can call me Gwen," she said.

"I don't like that name," he replied coldly.

"Would you like to change it?"

"I suppose I could call you Gwendolyn?"

"You can," she said. "Gwendolyn Anne Ashby, at your service."

"Miss Ashby it is, then."

Headmaster Yorke continued to stand on her porch looking handsome and grumpy all at once. She'd probably faint if she ever saw him smile. Such an occasion would be well worth the injury.

"I came here for a reason," he said finally.

"Did you?"

"Yes. I can't recall what it was, however."

"Was it to have tea with me?"

"I would never have tea with you. That would be highly—"

"Inappropriate?"

"Quite," he said.

"Of course it would. Tea is a well-known cause of inequity and concupiscence."

The headmaster's eyes widened.

"I'm an English teacher," she reminded him. "I know big words. Have you remembered why you came here yet?"

"Not yet."

"Maybe you're here to discuss how awkward it is that your students are trying to set us up?"

"No, it wasn't that."

"You wanted to do the gentlemanly thing and see how I was settling in? Ask me if I needed assistance or if you could make my stay here more comfortable?" Maybe make out with her on the sofa in the living room?

He glared at her for a moment longer, than asked how she was settling in, seemingly giving up on remembering the real reason he'd come to her cottage. "Can I assist you with anything?" he asked.

"No, I'm fine. I like it here. I thought I'd be bored with no internet and no television. But it's odd...I feel like I can think more clearly out here."

"One can hear oneself think out here. Although that's not always preferable."

Gwen leaned against the doorway and crossed her arms over her chest. "I guess as headmaster you have a lot on your mind all the time."

"I take care of thirty teenage boys."

Gwen laughed and nodded. "I thought you said sixty?"

He shook his head. "Thirty."

"Well, they're good kids. I can already tell."

"Thank you. I'm very proud of them."

"Do you have any kids of your own?" Gwen asked.

The headmaster shook his head. "The boys are more than enough for me."

"I would imagine so."

"I assume you have no children?"

"No, never been married," she said. "I love teaching children, so I sometimes feel like a parent, in a way. Except I get to send my kids home at the end of the day."

"No sending them home from here. They have their holidays but they're here year-round."

"And they like that? Being here year-round?"

"Many of them don't have a choice," he said. "Half the student body are orphans, like yourself. They're here on full scholarships. They have nowhere else to go."

"Half the students are orphans?" Gwen could scarcely believe it. "Even Laird?" She couldn't believe a boy with such a buoyant spirit had lost his family.

"No. But his situation is equally unfortunate. And entirely confidential. Needless to say, he wasn't safe at his previous home. He's safe now. I've seen to it."

"Can I say something?"

"I can't imagine I could stop you if I wanted to."

"I like you," she said.

"That's a terrible thing to say."

"Why?" Gwen asked, laughing.

"It's for the best if you don't like me, Miss Ashby. And it's certainly for the best if I don't like you."

"Because you're the headmaster here? It's okay. We can be friends, right?"

"The boys very much want you here. But they're young. Many of them have lost their mothers so they wish to have a woman on campus again. But they don't quite understand the sort of sacrifice you would have to make to stay here."

"Look, I know this place is a bit out of the way. And it's certainly a different kind of school than I've ever taught at. But it's not a sacrifice by any stretch of the imagination. All any teacher wants is a room full of intelligent and eager students and a principal who will trust her teaching methods."

"I haven't seen your teaching methods, Miss Ashby. I'm not easily impressed."

"Do you have any advice?"

"Pardon me?" Headmaster Yorke looked at her as if she'd suddenly grown a second head.

"I said, do you have any advice? You've been here ten years. You know all the students personally. Surely you have some advice," she said, hoping to steer him away from any conversations about her leaving the school.

"I do have advice. A plethora of advice."

"I'd love it if you shared your overflowing cornucopia of wisdom with me," Gwen said, trying to maintain a straight face. "Perhaps over tea in the kitchen?"

Headmaster Yorke wagged a finger at her. "You won't trick me that easily into drinking your tea of concupiscence, Miss Ashby."

She shrugged. "It was worth a shot."

"Have a pleasant evening. I'll leave you now so you can work on your lectures for next week."

"Oh, I'm finished with my lectures. I think I'll take a long, hot bath instead in that big, gorgeous bathtub," she said, hoping to annoy him. Was he picturing her wet and naked? She certainly would love to see him wet and naked. Or even just naked. She wasn't picky.

"You're a terrible person," Headmaster Yorke said. "The worst person I've ever met."

"Thank you," she said.

"You're fired."

"You can't fire me until you hire me."

"I'll hire you on Friday afternoon and then fire you. Good evening, Miss Ashby." And with that, Headmaster Yorke walked off without another word, leaving her alone on the porch.

"Play hard to get all you want," she said under her breath after he'd disappeared from view. "But you will be drinking tea with me before the week is over."

She went inside and shut the door. She paused with her hand on the lock. Seemed so silly to lock the door out here in the middle of nowhere. Then again, Headmaster Yorke had seemed genuinely concerned she was the only woman on campus. Perhaps he wasn't being so unreasonable. She turned the lock. Better safe than murdered by Jack the Ripper.

Gwen headed upstairs to the bathroom and ran hot water into the bathtub. She'd been teasing Headmaster Yorke with her bath talk, but once she'd said it, she knew that was exactly how she wanted to spend the rest of the evening.

Alone in her tub, buoyed by the steaming water, she imagined kissing Headmaster Yorke. She wouldn't call him Headmaster Yorke while they were kissing, would she? Only if he was into that sort of thing. Otherwise, it would be Edwin. She wondered what sort of kisser he was. Hard and passionate? Slow and gentle? Sexy and sizzling? All of the above?

Edwin hadn't corrected her when she mentioned the boys had told her about his divorce. Only he didn't seem the divorcing sort. More the "stick it out to the bitter end" sort. A lack of attraction seemed like the least plausible explanation for the divorce. Edwin Yorke was attractive and intelligent and employed—the holy trifecta of marriageable men. What woman in her right mind would kick him out of her life? She could only guess what had happened between husband and wife. Or she could guess until she got Edwin to tell her the whole story. And she would get the story out of him. She wanted to know everything about him—what he liked, what he hated, what his favorite song was, what his favorite food was, what he dreamed of at night...what he hoped for, longed for, and wanted in and out of bed.

"Edwin..." she whispered, slipping further underwater. What a wonderfully old English name. She'd love to moan it in his ear while he was deep inside her.

"Gwen, rein it in," she ordered herself. No more sexual fantasies about her gorgeous boss today. She'd hit her quota. The hot water on her naked body was giving her dangerous thoughts.

She wrapped herself in a plush white towel and stepped out of the tub and onto the tile. She had made sure the window blinds were closed earlier—the last thing she needed was for any of the students to see their new literature teacher naked. It was already hard enough to earn the trust and respect of teenagers. No need to exacerbate the situation by flashing the whole school.

Just in case she got more unexpected visitors, she put on her flannel pajamas instead of one of her skimpy nighties. Gwen pulled the covers down on the bed but paused before getting in. There was a smell...

Smoke. That was it. Smoke, acrid and caustic with a hint of death in it like roadkill baking on a hot highway.

Gwen rushed to the window, her first thought being that the surrounding forest was on fire. But no, she couldn't see any flames in the foothills. None of the buildings on campus were on fire, either. Was the smell coming from inside her cottage?

She ran downstairs and checked every room. The smell of smoke was strong, but she couldn't pinpoint its origin. Even the stove was cold.

As she climbed the stairs, the smell seemed to be dissipating. She'd talk to Headmaster Yorke about it tomorrow. Maybe something shady was going on out in the forest that she couldn't see? Someone burning garbage or a company illegally dumping chemicals? She didn't want any of the boys getting sick from that smell. It had certainly turned her stomach.

She returned to her bedroom and cracked the window. The smell, whatever it had been from, was gone.

One deep breath and the last traces in her nostrils vanished, replaced with fresh forest air.

Gwen closed her eyes and breathed in and out for a few minutes, relishing the clean, cool night breeze. She could smell the woods around her—the tree bark, the lush leaves, the rich, dark Carolina mountain soil. Peace returned to her heart. She would sleep the sleep of the dead tonight.

When Gwen re-opened her eyes, her whole body went cold with bright white terror.

A figure was gliding along the top of the twelve-foot-high brick wall that surrounded the school grounds, moving with the ease of a tightrope walker. Her first thought was that it was a ghost, glowing in the pale moonlight...but as her eyes focused, she could see that it was actually a woman in a white dress.

Headmaster Yorke had said Gwen was the only woman at this school. No female students. No female teachers.

The dress flowed to the woman's ankles in a haze of gossamer lace and silk. It looked like a wedding dress with heavy bell sleeves that hung past her hands. Gwen tried to make out her face, but it was hidden beneath a veil of lace and shadows.

Gwen shoved her feet into her shoes and raced from the bedroom and down the steps. Dammit, why did this school have to be in the middle of a telephone dead zone? She needed to call Edwin, the police, the entire world. The woman could be mentally ill or in some sort of distress. One misstep and the school could have a lawsuit on its hands. And what if the woman was dangerous? What if the woman had set the fire Gwen had smelled? She had no idea who this person was, but, even as a temporary employee, she had a duty to protect the students from harm.

She sprinted across the courtyard toward the figure in white, who was now moving faster along the wall.

"Hello?" Gwen called out.

No answer.

"Ma'am?" she called out again. "Miss?"

The distant cry of an animal spooked Gwen. She spun around, scanning the school grounds. An owl, probably. That was all.

When she turned her head back toward the wall, her mouth hung open in disbelief.

The woman was gone.

A figure was walking along the top of the twelve-foot-high brick wall that surrounded the school grounds... Her first thought was that it was a ghost, glowing in the pale moonlight....

CHAPTER SIX

That night Gwen could barely sleep. She lay in bed, wide awake. She couldn't get the image of the woman on the wall out of her mind. Who on earth could it have been? Where had she gone? The walls that surrounded the school were ivy- and moss-covered. Who would scramble up those slick, dirty walls wearing white?

There had to be a logical explanation. Gwen believed in a lot of things—love, hope, the power of a cup of hot tea to make everything better—but ghosts? Not a chance.

Maybe one of the boys had a girlfriend who snuck into the school to visit him? But where would she have come from? Had she climbed in from the outside, or strolled through the front gate? Anyone wanting to be clandestine would have worn dark colors and stuck to the shadows. This girl had worn bright white and paraded along the wall...

As soon as the clock ticked past 8:00 a.m., Gwen gave

up on sleep. She got out of bed and dressed for the day. In her tan slacks and white blouse, she was the picture of day-off propriety. She didn't want the headmaster accusing her of trying to entice him into drinking tea with her by wearing a scandalous outfit. No man in the history of the world had ever been seduced by a woman in tan slacks.

Gwen wasn't in the mood for flirting today.

She wanted answers.

She marched up to the fourth floor of the main building and knocked on the headmaster's office door. He didn't answer. She hadn't really expected him to be in his office on a Sunday morning. She'd felt beyond uncomfortable knocking on the door to his private quarters, but that was exactly what she would have to do now. She had no choice, not where the safety of the boys was concerned.

She knocked at his door and stepped back. After a short wait, she heard footsteps inside.

"You," Headmaster Yorke said, finally opening the door. He was dressed in black trousers, a white shirt, a black and gray tie, and a black-and-grey vest. All that was missing was his jacket.

"Me?" she asked, momentarily taken aback.

"You are tenacious. I thought we already discussed the tea issue—"

"Forget tea. I think I saw a ghost," she said. "Well, not a ghost. Just a person who was there one second and then wasn't there the next and everything about the whole thing defied explanation."

"But not a ghost?"

"Right."

Headmaster Yorke stared at her a moment. This morning he looked handsome as ever. His midnight-blue eyes wore an inscrutable expression behind his glasses.

"Come in," he said. "I've just put the kettle on."

They sat in his small but refined kitchen. It was the sort of kitchen one would see on an English soap opera set in the Art Deco era. Hercule Poirot's kitchen—that was what it was. He poured her a cup of weak black tea—weak by her standards, anyway—in a square teacup set on a square saucer. She did love the Art Deco style, even if it made for an odd drinking angle.

"Is there a reason for the square teacups?" she asked.

"I have a fondness for ninety-degree angles," Headmaster Yorke said. He poured a splash of milk into his tea and stirred it with a dainty silver spoon that looked like a baby spoon in his large hands. "Now tell me what you saw."

"I saw a woman in white."

"You weren't reading Wilkie Collins in the bath, were you?"

"No, I was not. And this wasn't *that* woman in white. She was…I don't know. She was weird. But definitely there. Sort of. Until she wasn't. I promise I'm not crazy. I saw her."

"I believe you."

"You do?"

"Of course I do," Headmaster Yorke said.

"Because I'm so honest and you trust me that much?"

"No. Because you talk so much I doubt you've had enough time to come up with such an elaborate story."

She pursed her lips at him. "I don't talk that much. Do I?"

He smiled slightly behind his teacup with all its admirable ninety-degree angles.

"Mr. Yorke, I'm not kidding here. There's literally a strange woman wandering around the school at night," she said, her voice solemn. "She might try to hurt one of the boys. I mean, walking on a wall at night doesn't seem like the sanest sort of behavior. She might need help, you know?"

"You needn't worry about the boys. The woman in white hasn't harmed anyone yet, and I'm quite certain she doesn't mean to harm anyone—now or ever. Or herself."

Gwen gaped at him. "So you know about her."

"I do."

"Well, who is she? What's she doing there?"

"I can't say who she is. She's seen on campus at night sometimes. You might see her again. You may not. That is all. No need to fret."

"Oh, I'm fretting. I'm definitely fretting. How long has she been doing this?"

"For a while now," he said. "The boys call her the Bride since it appears she's wearing a wedding dress."

"We need to work on their creative-naming skills."

"Perhaps. But they've lost interest in her. They've even given up trying to catch her. And so should you."

"From the way she moved, she appeared young. Does she live near here?"

"No one has ever spoken to her. The boys like to think she's a ghost."

"A ghost? Really?" Gwen asked, disappointed that such an outlandish explanation was his only explanation. "She certainly appeared ghost-like at first. But I don't believe in ghosts."

"The boys believe in ghosts. Then again, boys enjoy believing in ghosts. It's something safe to be afraid of, something safe to say you aren't afraid of."

An astute assessment. She recalled her elementary school days. A few abandoned shacks had sat at the corner of the school lot. Supposedly a dozen people were murdered in one of the shacks and the madman buried the bodies in the basement. The students would dare each other to run up and touch the house. The story was all lies and nonsense, of course. Children loved to scare each other. She could easily believe the boys badly wanted the woman in white to be a ghost.

"You don't believe she's a ghost, do you?" she asked the headmaster.

"No, of course not. But I don't tell that to the students. They enjoy coming up with theories on her identity."

"What's the reigning theory?"

"Once there was a fire in this area that killed several people. She might have died in the fire, and now she walks at night."

"I smelled smoke last night," Gwen said. "Not that it had anything to do with the woman, I suppose…"

Headmaster Yorke refilled his teacup. "I don't recall any of the boys ever saying they smelled smoke in her presence."

"I thought maybe someone was burning trash near-by," Gwen offered.

"The school is the only residence in the woods for miles around. But the wind carries scents long distances. I think I've even smelled the ocean a time or two when the air is clear."

Gwen picked up her tea and drank a sip. "So the boys think she's a ghost. You don't think she's a ghost. Who is she, then?"

"If there was cause for concern, I promise I would be concerned. Let it go."

"Do I have to?" she asked.

"If you don't, I'll take your tea away."

"Fine. I'll let it go," she said. "For now."

After finishing her tea, Headmaster Yorke escorted her to the door.

"Can we have tea again soon?" she asked.

"Absolutely never."

"So wine then?"

He didn't even deign to reply to that with anything but a glare.

"Water? Would you share a thimble of water with me?" she teased.

"Are we in a desert and it's the last thimble of water on Earth?" he asked.

"Yes, we are, and yes, it is."

He paused as if giving the question serious consideration.

"No."

He shut the door in her face—gently, leaving at least four inches between the wood and her nose. Gwen stared at the closed door. She couldn't figure Edwin Yorke out to save her life. He'd called her lovely...but wouldn't call her

Gwen. He refused to have tea with her...but then invited her in for tea. What a mystery. What a puzzle. She had to solve him. A challenge, yes, but one she relished.

Cary had never been a challenge. He'd been easy, simple. They had been friends for a year before they'd gone out on their first date. Falling in love had been gradual and lazy. She'd loved him because he'd made it easy to love him. She hadn't been able to think of any reason not to love him. So she'd loved him because loving a good man who was hardworking and kind was the sensible thing to do. There had never been much passion in the relationship. They were friends who shared a bed. When he left her, she missed him but not enough to think for one second that she should have followed him across the ocean.

All those feelings about Cary belonged to a past life now. A life she'd already started to forget.

Then there was the headmaster...

Her attraction to Headmaster Yorke had been instantaneous, overwhelming, and irrepressible. And honestly obnoxious. He was taking over her brain and there didn't seem to be anything she could do about it. She didn't like being this out of control of her emotions.

Except she kind of did like it. She swore she'd never seen a more attractive man in her life. Even his rudeness endeared him to her. The more he pretended to dislike her, the more she liked him. She could feel their attraction was mutual, but sensed the good heart in him wouldn't let him act out of an overdeveloped sense of propriety. And just because the students wanted them together didn't mean they would be hopping into bed.

Well, not yet anyway.

She'd wait until she officially got the job.

By Sunday evening, she'd mostly forgotten about the mysterious bride. She trusted Headmaster Yorke. If he said the Bride wasn't a threat to the school, she would believe him.

That didn't mean she would stop trying to figure out who she was and what she was doing skulking around the school.

———

Gwen slept the sleep of the angels that night, and woke up refreshed and invigorated Monday morning. A bell rang—the start of the school day. She dressed in her best grey skirt and blouse and matching kitten heels.

She put all her notes into a portfolio, stuffed it into her messenger bag, and strode with more confidence than she felt to her classroom. Every one of the ten boys in her first class of the day were on time and sitting in their seats.

"Good morning, gentlemen," she greeted them.

They all stared at her in silence.

"You all can talk," she said. "I mean, one at a time."

They remained silent, but she saw them giving each other the side-eye, daring someone, anyone, to speak first.

"Are you all this well-trained or just terrified?"

No answer.

"Okay, both obviously," she said. "All right, let's try this. Laird?"

"Ma'am?"

"Ah, a human voice. Better. How are you?"

"Fine and dandy, Miss Ashby," he answered with a jaunty little salute.

"Wonderful, Laird." She turned her attention to the boy sitting next to him. "Christopher? How are you?"

"Fine, Miss Ashby," he said, his voice squeaking a little.

"Very good. I'm going to try to learn everyone's names. I may need you all to help me out a little."

The ten boys each took a piece of paper out of a notebook and scribbled something across it. Gwen watched with curiosity as they all folded the papers in half and set them up on the edge of their wooden desks. Nameplates. They'd all created nameplates.

"All right," she said as she now had all their names in front of her. "That's handy. Thank you."

"We had to do that for Miss Muir," Christopher said.

"Smart lady. I hope I can fill her shoes."

"You can," Laird said. "Your feet are bigger than hers."

The whole class tittered with laughter.

"Boys," came a male voice from the door. "Let's give Miss Ashby our attention and respect."

Headmaster Yorke was standing in the doorway, his hands in his jacket pockets. He appeared to be actively repressing the urge to glower. It seemed to be his best attempt at looking casual and relaxed. It was, to say the least, a total failure.

"What are you doing here?" Gwen asked, her words coming out more accusatory than she'd intended.

"I'm Headmaster. I'm observing. Carry on. Pretend I'm not here."

"All right everyone, get under your desks. It's nap time."

The class burst into laughter. Laird was already under his desk.

"Miss Ashby?" Headmaster Yorke intoned.

"What? You said to pretend you weren't here."

She smiled at him, a smile he didn't return.

"Just kidding," she told the class. "No napping. Let's get started. I thought we'd read *Great Expectations* this week. Charles Dickens. Any Dickens fans here?"

All the boys raised their hands.

"Lying liars. I refuse to believe *all* of you are Dickens fans."

"We read *A Tale of Two Cities* last term," Laird said. "It was a ripping good yarn."

"*A Tale of Two Cities*?" she repeated. "Pretty impressive. I didn't read that until college."

"Marshal Students," Headmaster Yorke began, "are given a university-level education here at the pre-university level. You can challenge them, Miss Ashby. I assure you they can keep up."

Gwen drummed her fingers on her desk. "Really?"

"He means it," Christopher said. "Try us."

Well, that was a challenge she couldn't resist.

"Try you? This should be fun." Gwen glanced at Headmaster Yorke, who waved his hand at the class. He seemed to be daring her as much as the boys were.

"What's the significance of the year 1623 in English literature?" she asked. "Anyone?"

Christopher raised his hand. "First Folio," he said when she pointed at him. "That was the year thirty-six of Shakespeare's works were collected and printed. If that hadn't happened, Shakespeare's plays might have been lost to the world."

"They'd been printed before," Laird said.

"Yes, but the First Folio has the only definitive text of about twenty of the plays," Christopher countered. "People would sit in the audience and take dictation. The texts were a mess."

"A veritable Shakespearean tragedy," Gwen agreed. "Why is Dante's greatest work known as *The Divine Comedy* when it's not at all a comedy?"

"I don't know about that," Laird said. "I laughed at the scene with the man carrying his severed head like a lantern. He raises his head up in his hand to see better."

"I wouldn't call poor Bertran de Born a laugh riot," she said. "Although it is a striking image."

A young man raised his hand and Gwen called on him. His nameplate read SAMUEL. He was, regrettably, the only Black student she'd seen on campus.

"All works of literature," Samuel said, "were divided into the two classic genres of comedy and tragedy. A tragedy ended in a death. A comedy ended in a marriage. Since no one dies at the end and Dante the Pilgrim is closer to God at the end, Dante the Writer considered it a comedy."

"Correct," Miss Ashby said. "Who can tell me the year the first Bible was produced in English?"

A boy named Steven answered that question. 1526 by William Tyndale. Another student—Jefferson, who had a deep Georgia drawl—recited the entire Gettysburg Address for them and put the speech into its historical context. She threw ten more questions at the students, quizzing them on things she'd learned in either college or while working on her master's degree. The boys answered correctly and without hesitation. It was like they'd spent their entire lives in school.

"Okay," she said, nodding her head. "I'm convinced. There's not a young man in this room who couldn't go off to any college in the country tomorrow and excel there."

"You've barely even scratched the surface, Miss Ashby," Headmaster Yorke said. "Watch this. Gentlemen, *virescit vulnere virtus.*"

"Courage flourishes beyond from a wound," the boys translated.

"*Quoniam diu vixesse denegatur, aliquid faciamus quo possimus ostendere nos vixisse,*" Headmaster Yorke said.

"As length of life is denied to us, we should at least do something to show that we have lived," the boys answered.

"And who are we quoting? Laird?"

"Cicero," Laird answered.

"*Homines, dum docent, discunt.* Alan?"

"Men learn while they teach. Seneca."

Headmaster Yorke shot Gwen a pointed look.

"Women, too," she said.

"I don't know the Latin for that," Alan said. "Sorry."

"I forgive you," she said.

"*Deficit omne quod nasciture,*" Headmaster Yorke said.

"Everything that is born passes away. Quintilian," a blond boy named Stanley translated.

"And one final one in French," Headmaster Yorke said. *"Tous pour un, un pour tous."*

"All for one and one for all!" the boys shouted with gusto.

Gwen applauded. "Great job. That's wonderful."

"This school was founded on the classical principles of virtue, wisdom, and duty," Headmaster Yorke said. "Faithfulness, loyalty, striving through hardship, and brotherhood are what Marshal students embody. An educated populace lifts an entire community, an entire country. Learning is a civic duty. One of these young gentlemen might be the next Dr. Salk discovering the vaccine for the next polio. They understand that they aren't learning to merely uplift themselves or to impress a teacher, but learning to change and improve the world that gave them life."

"Although," Jefferson with the Georgia accent said, "we do like impressing the teachers."

"I'm beyond impressed," Gwen said. "I'm honored to have a chance to teach you."

"Then carry on," Headmaster Yorke said, beaming like a proud father at his boys.

"With pleasure," Gwen said. She passed out the copies of *Great Expectations* she'd picked up at the library. "I think you'll all like this book. Christopher, will you read the first page for us?"

And so it began. Christopher started to read and the class listened with rapt attention. She gave them a short biographical sketch of Charles Dickens, his wife, and his many, many children. A prolific man in several respects— fifteen books, ten children.

Under his breath, Laird muttered, "Bet his wife was as sore as his hand."

Gwen pretended not to hear that.

The first day of class went better than she'd dreamed. The students asked interesting questions about Dickens and the story they were reading. *What did the title mean? Dickens wrote many young characters. Did he write the books for his children to read? Why did he give Pip the worst name in literary history?* Gwen reminded the boys that in the nineteenth century, the word "pip" was a common synonym for the seeds found inside fruit. She could almost see the little light bulbs switching on over their heads, the name suddenly holding new significance for them.

At the end of class, Gwen assigned the first five chapters of the book to the boys to read that night. The headmaster had said Marshal students thrived on challenges, and she was pleasantly surprised to see a distinct lack of eye-rolling as she announced the assignment. Either they enjoyed reading books as much as she did, or they simply had nothing else to do out here in the middle of nowhere.

The boys filed out of her class at the sound of the bell. They were loud but orderly. She kept waiting to hear profanities but the boys kept a civil tongue. Once the classroom was empty of students, Headmaster Yorke approached her desk.

"A good first class," he said. "You kept their attention. And mine."

"Thank you. I love the book. I think that helps."

"You won't always be able to teach books you love."

"I don't know. I love to read. I'm sure I can find something to love in almost any work of literature. Except maybe *Crime and Punishment.* Never learned to love that one."

"It's a bit grim," Headmaster Yorke agreed. "Most Russian literature is."

"I promise I won't foist *Anna Karenina* on the boys. Not this week anyway."

"I shall thank you on behalf of the students for that act of mercy."

"You're welcome. I'll teach them *War and Peace* instead," she said with a wink.

"They would read all fourteen-hundred pages of it if you asked them to, Miss Ashby."

"I doubt that. They'd do it for you, though."

"Nonsense," the headmaster said.

"I saw them trying to impress you today," she said. "You're their hero."

"Hero? Me? Hardly. Shakespeare is their hero. Cicero. Sir William Marshal, whom this school is named after, is their hero."

"They adore you. I've never seen anything like it. They wanted to make you proud."

"They did make me proud. They always make me proud."

"I hope I can make you proud, too," she said.

"Keep up the good work and perhaps you will." He gave her a slight smile, enough of a smile to make her blush.

"I should get ready for my next class," Gwen said. "It's nice that this is such a small school. I can give the students so much more attention."

"They thrive with personal attention. Russell has a

little trouble with reading comprehension. You should make him read aloud. If he reads aloud, he remembers nearly everything he reads. But if he reads silently to himself, he retains very little of it."

"That's good to know. Is there anything else I need to know about the students?"

"A great deal."

"Maybe we should talk about them in depth. Tonight. Over dinner," she said.

Headmaster Yorke stared down at her. Gwen pasted on a bright smile in an attempt to look innocent.

"You are merciless," he said. "And stubborn."

"I'm not asking you for anything inappropriate—like tea."

"No tea?"

"No tea and no concupiscence. I promise. Just dinner and discussing matters relevant to the students."

"Well...as long as we discuss only matters relevant to the students..."

"I'm sure you have dinner with Mr. Price and Mr. Reynolds on occasion, yes?"

"Yes."

"Then wouldn't it be odd if you and I didn't have dinner together? Wouldn't it be as if you were giving me special treatment in the form of neglect?"

"We can't have anyone thinking I'm singling you out."

"No, we can't." Gwen nearly batted her eyelashes at him but thought that would be overdoing it. "In all seriousness," she continued, forcing herself back to the topic, "I want to be the teacher these boys need. It's a work dinner. That's all. We don't even have to look at each other. We can sit back-to-back and talk."

"Very well," he said. He pointed his finger at her. "Work talk only. And I'm only allowing you to have dinner with me because I want my students to have the best possible education. It isn't because I like you and enjoy your company."

"Of course not."

"Although I do."

Gwen smiled up at him. "Dinner at eight?"

"That would be fine. But no tea."

"No tea at all," she promised.

"Good."

"I'll bring wine instead," she said, though if there was a wine cellar on campus she hadn't yet found it.

The headmaster only shook his head and walked away.

Gwen would have liked to stay at the door and watch him walk away. He looked almost as good from the back as he did from the front.

But she had things to do.

Teach the next group of students.

Eat some lunch.

Get ready for dinner with the headmaster.

She didn't care what he said about only discussing students. That was all smoke and mirrors. She knew it. He knew it. They both knew it. This wasn't a work dinner.

This was a date.

CHAPTER SEVEN

Gwen's second class went as well as her first, and her third class even better. With such a small student body, every class was like an intimate conversation instead of herding cattle like her old teaching job had been. These kids had manners, real manners, old-fashioned manners. Someone—the headmaster, most likely—had drilled good behavior into them. She'd be sure to thank him for that unexpected gift tonight.

Tonight... She was having dinner with the headmaster tonight. She fully intended to be on her best behavior. No flirting. No teasing. She'd hate for the headmaster to think she was willing to sleep her way into a full-time job at the school.

Still, when it came time to dress for dinner, she put on her favorite dress (which also happened to be her only dress). It had been a vintage shop find, dark blue velvet that came down to her knees but just barely. She put on a choker and matching headband. As she examined her reflection in the mirror, she realized she looked like she was on her way to a cotillion in 1964. Not a bad look. She hoped the headmaster would approve.

She grabbed a sweater and, with some trepidation, headed out at five before eight toward Hawkwood Hall. Were the boys watching her? She was certain of it. Did they know where she was going? Where else would she be going looking like this—the library?

Maybe dinner with the headmaster had been a bad idea. Too late. There was no backing out now.

She headed up to the top floor and raised her hand to knock on his door, equal parts nervous and excited. Here it was again—a new path in front of her. Everything in her told her to go for it. Everything else told her to run back. But back where? Her old life was gone. All that waited for her outside this school was a couch in Chicago. Nothing to lose. Everything to gain.

She knocked.

Headmaster Yorke opened the door. At first, she hardly recognized him. He was wearing the same suit from earlier, without his jacket. But it wasn't his clothes that confused her. It was his face.

"Where are your glasses?" she asked, seeing his naked face for the first time.

"I don't need glasses to eat dinner," he said, welcoming her into his private residence.

"You look so different," she said, studying his face with unabashed curiosity.

"Is something the matter with my face?" he asked.

"I thought your eyes were dark blue, but they're more dark green, aren't they?"

"I don't know. I've never checked."

She rolled her eyes. "I don't believe that for a minute. Everyone knows what color their eyes are."

"They most certainly do not," he said as he escorted her to the dining room. Dinner was already laid out on fine white china. Two tall taper candles illuminated the table. Shockingly, he'd found a bottle of wine for them.

"Unless somebody's blind, they know what color their eyes are," Gwen said as Headmaster Yorke pulled out her chair. She sat down and tucked her skirt around her knees. "You have to know for your driver's license."

"I simply never paid attention to it."

"You're teasing me. I know you are."

"Fine," he said, uncorking and pouring the white wine. "What color are your eyes?"

"Blue," she said. "Boring old blue."

"My point is proven." He sat opposite her and laid his napkin across his lap. "You don't have blue eyes at all."

She smiled at his accent. *At all* sounded like *a'tall*. She wished she had a phone book so she could make him read from it.

"They're blue," she insisted. "I've seen them. More than once."

"I'm afraid you're mistaken. They are azure, a common color used in heraldry. Azure is a jewel tone. It also represents Jupiter. It is a noble color carried on the crest by noble French houses. To call your eyes blue would be to call an emerald 'green' or a ruby 'red.' An emerald is emerald. A ruby is ruby. Your eyes are azure. I've seen the crown jewels, and they sparkle less than your eyes do. So there," he said. "You are wrong. I am correct. Now eat your dinner."

Gwen sat speechless at the table while Headmaster Yorke lifted his wineglass and took a sip. She placed her napkin back onto the table and stood up.

"What are you doing, Miss Ashby? I believe I told you to eat your dinner."

She came to his end of the table and took his wineglass from his hand. "I will," she said. "I have to do something first."

"What?" he asked with extreme suspiciousness.

"This." She bent down and kissed him. As their lips touched, she felt a current pass through her, the smallest bolt of lightning. The surface of her skin crackled with excitement.

"That was a foolish thing to do," Edwin said. Now that she'd kissed him, she could only think of him as Edwin.

"Was it?"

"Yes."

"So I shouldn't do it again?"

"I didn't say that."

Smiling, Gwen returned to her seat and laid her napkin across her lap. "You are a very strange man," she said.

"You don't know the half of it. Now eat before I send you home without supper."

They ate. They talked. They mostly stayed on the subject and the subject was the Marshal Academy.

Unfortunately. Gwen wanted to know everything

about Edwin Yorke, but the one thing she was learning about Edwin Yorke tonight was that Edwin Yorke did not like talking about himself.

Must have been a British thing.

"I really don't see why the boys object to *Ivanhoe* so vociferously," he was saying. "When I was their age, I couldn't read it enough. Wonderful writing."

"So I get nothing?" she asked after they'd finished their second glass of wine.

"Silence, maiden; thy tongue outruns thy discretion."

"Excuse me?" Gwen said.

"That was a line from *Ivanhoe*."

She glared at him. "You're driving me insane."

He set his now empty glass aside and studied her from across the table. "What exactly is it that you want from me, Miss Ashby?"

"Well...for starters, I want you to call me Gwen."

He sighed heavily. So heavily she had to laugh.

"Gwen," he said once and only once.

"Now that didn't hurt, did it?"

"I wouldn't say it hurt."

"Good."

"It might have chafed, however."

"Edwin," she chided him.

He glared at her.

"You called me Gwen," she said. "That's tacit permission for me to call you by your first name."

"Very well. But only until this wine wears off."

"While the wine is wearing on...tell me about yourself. Please?" She added the *please* at the end so it would sound more like a humble request and less like an order. She didn't want to push her luck.

"What is it, precisely, that you want to know about me?"

"What are you doing here?"

"I live here, Gwen," he said in a tone so dry she could have used it to sand the paint from a dresser.

"You know what I mean. What's a man from England doing living in the foothills of the Appalachian Mountains?"

"Working."

"You're not going to give up anything to me here, are you?"

"This was supposed to be a work dinner. You should limit the scope of your questions to matters school-related."

"Tell me about the school's headmaster then. What should I know about him? As a teacher, I mean."

Edwin narrowed his eyes at her across the table. Four feet of table lay between them and it was four feet too many.

"Fine. Fine. Fine," she said, raising her hands in surrender. "Tell me this, then. You originally told me there were sixty students here before correcting yourself. Why?"

Edwin looked to the side. It was the first time she'd seen him refusing to make eye contact with her.

"Edwin?" Gwen prompted. His unwillingness to answer made the question all that much more important.

"I did something last year that caused a few parents and guardians to remove their children from the school.

Forgive me if I misspoke. It's been difficult to accept their loss."

"You did something? What on earth could you have done to scare off thirty students?"

"I assure you the students wanted to stay. To say there was wailing and gnashing of teeth when they were taken away would be only a minor exaggeration."

"Then what did you do to make the families pull their kids out of the school?"

"I integrated Marshal."

Gwen boggled at him for what must have been a full thirty seconds.

"Samuel," she said.

Edwin nodded.

"Half the school left because you let in Samuel? What the fuck?"

"Gwendolyn!"

"Sorry," she said reflexively, before correcting herself with a slap on the table. "No, I'm not sorry. That's worthy of an f-bomb."

"Thank God the children aren't here."

"They aren't children. They're teenagers. I'm sure they've heard and said worse. Now tell me you're joking. I know we're in the South, but that's insane."

"I wouldn't joke about such a thing. Ever. I only wish I were joking. Samuel wrote the school last year asking if he'd be welcome here. His IQ is off the charts and he was having trouble at his high school in Alabama. Not enough stimulation. Too much bullying. I sent him an entrance exam. He passed with the highest score in the history of the school. I offered him a full scholarship. He arrived and..."

"I can't believe this. Well, unfortunately, I can, but still...this isn't the 1950s, right?"

"Samuel offered to leave. I told him I would shut the school down before I would allow that. So he stayed. Thirty students were pulled out by their families. In the end, perhaps it was for the best... *Non, je ne regrette rien.*"

"Is that also from *Ivanhoe*?"

"Édith Piaf. Are you all right?"

"Yes. No. In shock."

Half the student body gone in one stroke. And Edwin was right, of course. He'd made the only choice he could have, especially for a man with his inherent sense of fairness and integrity. He'd done the only thing he could have done.

And now she would do the only thing she could do in response.

Gwen stood up, walked around the table, bent over, and kissed him on the mouth.

Again.

This time, instead of returning to her chair, she waited for a response.

"That was a shameful display," Edwin said, throwing his napkin down on the table.

"Was it?" she asked, suddenly nervous.

"Worst kiss in the history of kisses."

"What? You think you can do better?"

"With my eyes closed."

"Isn't that how everybody—"

Edwin rose, cupped the back of her neck, and kissed her right into the history books.

It was a deep kiss, a hard kiss, a strong kiss that made her weak. She wrapped her arms around his shoulders and pressed her breasts to his chest, a move that sent a soft moan escaping his lips. Or hers. She couldn't tell and certainly didn't care. How could she care now that Edwin was pushing her back against the wall? A man so reserved, so buttoned-up and aloof, had to have a breaking point.

Thank God she'd finally found it.

"Edwin," she whispered against his mouth, feeling a jolt of pleasure in her stomach at merely saying his name. He said nothing in response. Nothing could distract his lips from hers. She raised her head to give him better access to her neck. He took it, dropping a line of kisses that left her shivering from her jaw to her ear. He nipped at her neck and she gasped from the pleasure of his teeth against her skin.

"More," she begged.

He pulled away a few inches and grasped her waist with both of his large hands. She arched her back and he kissed her across her chest under her collarbone. She wanted him to strip her naked, put her on the table, send the dishes flying, and bury himself inside her. How desperately she wanted him inside her...but Edwin held back and merely teased her with his hands over her dress, not under it where she wanted them.

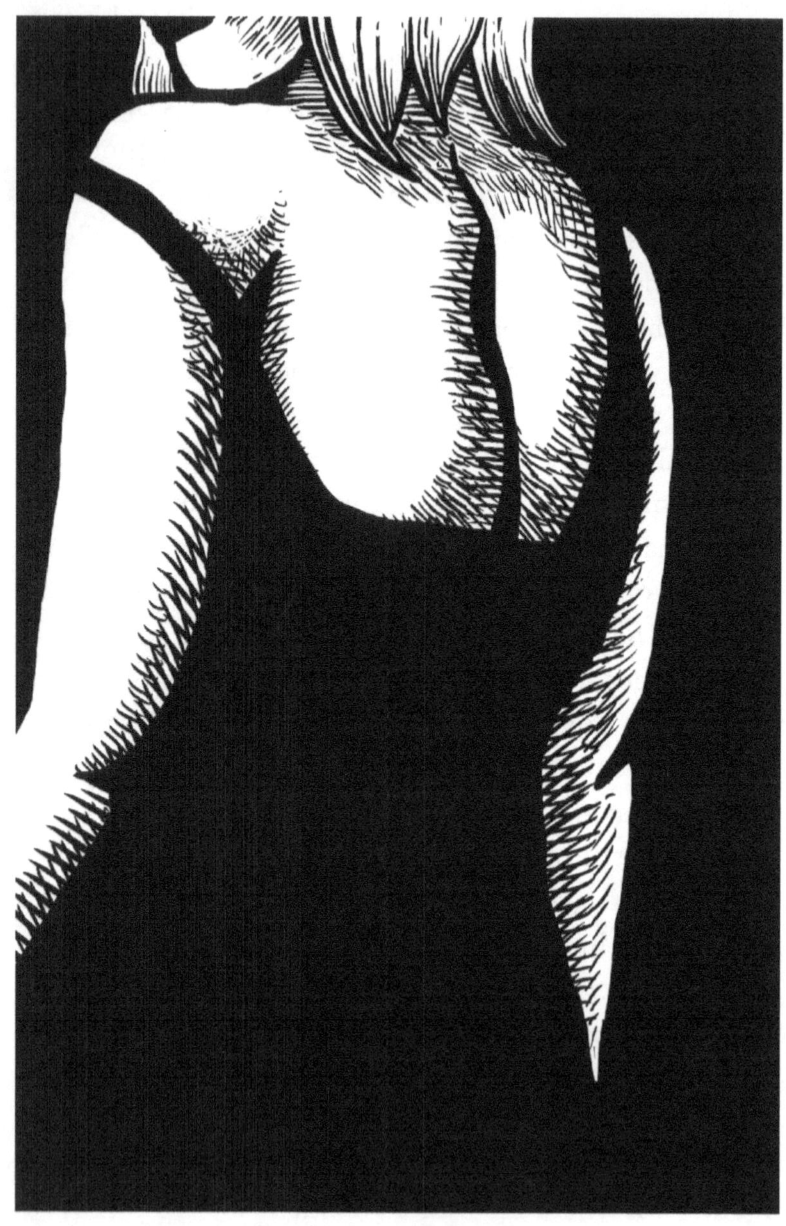

*She gasped as he pulled her dress down her left arm
and kissed her bare shoulder.*

She gasped as he pulled her dress down her left arm and kissed her bare shoulder. But it wasn't enough to let him kiss her. She dug her fingers into the knot of his tie and loosened it. If she didn't get to his neck soon, she would die. With a fierce pull, his tie was on the floor where it belonged. She unbuttoned the top two buttons of his shirt and buried her lips in the hollow of his throat.

Her pulse beat hard and fast. She felt his incredible hardness pressing against the center of her stomach as she kissed his neck and chest. Gwen pushed her hips into his and Edwin grunted softly in her ear. She'd never heard a more erotic sound than that tiny, uncontrolled release of pleasure. His fingers tightened with bruising force on her back. How could mere kissing feel this good, this powerful? She was ready to come apart in his arms any moment now.

"Make love to me, Edwin," she whispered in his ear.

And just like that, the spell was broken. The kiss ended so quickly she nearly fell to her knees when she lost the support of his arms. She grasped the wall for support. Edwin took another step back.

"What?" Gwen asked, panting. "What is it?"

"I apologize for my behavior," he said, buttoning up his shirt.

"Apologize for kissing me?" she asked, still too shocked to think clearly.

"I think it would be best if you leave, Miss Ashby."

She stared at him, utterly flabbergasted and deeply wounded. "My name is Gwen."

"I think you should leave, Miss Ashby," he said again. "I am the headmaster of this school. You are a teacher here. At least for this week. We should behave accordingly."

Gwen adjusted her sweater to cover herself up again and took a deep steadying breath.

"I was joking before when I said I didn't like you," she said. "I'm not joking now. You won't even talk to me about this?"

"There's nothing to talk about."

"You had your tongue in my mouth thirty seconds ago and now you're telling me to leave."

"I apologize for that."

"This...this was ungentlemanly of you," she said, and knew from the look in his eyes that her insult had struck deep.

She turned her back on him and walked out. On the third floor, she was mentally listing all the reasons she hated him. On the second floor, she started berating herself for kissing him first. On the first floor, she had to stop in the bathroom to wipe the tears off her face.

For a miserable half hour, she lingered in the bathroom until she'd achieved an approximation of composure again. She had a feeling several of the boys had seen her walking to the headmaster's. If they saw her leaving with her lips swollen and tears on her face, they might assume he had done something untoward to her. As angry as she was at him, she didn't want anyone thinking he'd harmed her. No harm at all. He'd only crushed her pride with his sudden coldness. She asked him to make love to her, and he'd pushed her away as if she'd confessed to a murder. He'd even apologized for kissing her, which was the cruelest blow of all. A man only apologized when he thought he'd done something wrong, something he regretted. It had been the most passionate, sensuous, and carnal kiss of her life, and he'd apologized for it.

Once she was entirely certain that she could pass for calm and rational, Gwen left the bathroom and walked back to her cottage under the nearly full moon.

She brewed a pot of tea and sat at the kitchen table pondering what had gone wrong. Edwin was divorced, so she knew he'd been with at least one woman in his life. As obsessed as he was with gentlemanly conduct and propriety, she might have guessed he was a virgin had she not known about his previous marriage. Before this evening, she'd found his old-fashioned manners charming and eccentric. Now they hurt and infuriated her.

Gwen did her best to focus on her work that night. She read, she made notes, and she thought of interesting topics of discussion for class the next day. When she finally retired for the evening, she barely slept. This time, she had no mysterious bride to blame.

———

HER MOOD BRIGHTENED when she got into her classroom the next day. The boys in her first class were ready to talk. Every last one of them had read the chapters she'd assigned and all ten boys participated in the discussion.

Laird thought it interesting that Pip loved someone as coldhearted as Estella. Gwen posited that people tended to want what they couldn't have, even if it was bad for them.

"Like me and dairy foods," Jefferson said. "Not a good combination."

"Tell us about it," Laird said, pinching his own nose.

Gwen kept waiting for Edwin to show up and observe her like he had done yesterday, but he never once showed his face. Not for her first class, her second class, or her afternoon class.

Long after the last boy had shuffled out of her classroom, she was sitting at her desk going through her notes when an apple suddenly appeared on her desk.

She looked up and saw Laird smiling kindly down at her.

"For you, Miss Ashby," he said. "There's an orchard behind the school. Thought you might need this."

She held the big red apple in her hand. "Thank you, Laird. I appreciate that."

"Give him time," Laird said in a low conspiratorial tone. "He's out of practice around women."

"You're playing matchmaker again."

"They say every Adam needs his Eve," he said with a wink and left her alone with her apple.

She took a big bite out of it, pretending it was Edwin's heart.

———

WEDNESDAY PROCEEDED SIMILARLY TO TUESDAY, without an appearance from the headmaster in her classroom. Did he trust her to do her job, or was he avoiding her? She and Edwin hadn't spoken since Monday night when they'd shared that life-altering kiss…life-altering for her, at least.

After her final class, Gwen headed out the back door of Hawkwood Hall. She needed to walk, to stretch her legs, and to think.

Gwen was a sensible soul, always had been. Whenever the world had fallen apart around her, she'd remained calm and rational. When had she ever lost her heart—and her mind—like this over a man? What was wrong with her? She was acting as if one kiss was the difference between life and death.

She had to come to her senses. Was any kiss worth giving up her life for? Staying at a school out in the middle of nowhere with no internet access, a single landline phone, and a headmaster who made her every kind of irrational, imprudent, and insensible?

No, she couldn't make decisions with her heart and her body. She needed to use her brain. And her brain told her that she shouldn't stay at a school where she had such strong feelings for the headmaster.

So why didn't she leave?

Gwen strolled along the perimeter of the school inside the wall. For such a small school, it boasted a relatively large campus. The five buildings stood on a square quarter-mile of land. From the looks of it, it would take her twenty minutes simply to walk one lap around campus, past each of the four turrets where the walls were joined.

She studied the ground as she walked the length of the wall, searching for...what? Any clues that the Bride was more than a phantom? She already knew that, though. Besides, there wasn't much in the way of evidence for her to inspect. The dirt and grass were disturbed from the boys' rough-housing; the only shoe prints she came across were clearly too large to be the woman's.

At the third turret, the one that faced northwest, Gwen discovered a narrow staircase built into the wall. She carefully walked up the stone stairs and discovered a small room inside what she'd assumed had been a merely decorative feature. It had a narrow opening, so narrow she had to slide in sideways.

Inside the turret, she discovered nothing but some dust and bits of paper. Apparently, the boys liked to do their homework out here. She found some equations, a few Latin quotes...

But what was this?

Gwen unfolded a sheet of notebook paper.

Saturday night. Usual place. Please, I want you.

Gwen grinned as she read the note. Steam practically rose off those eight little words.

Her theory that one of the boys had a secret girlfriend who was sneaking onto campus didn't seem so farfetched now.

For two whole seconds, Gwen considered taking the note to Edwin. Surely bringing a girl onto campus was a huge violation of the rules. But she was no snitch, and Edwin had already chosen to turn a blind eye to the Bride for whatever reason.

She tore the note into tiny pieces.

————

THE REST of the week felt like swimming in the ocean. Working with the boys buoyed Gwen's spirits but being ignored by Edwin left her drowning in confusion. So she focused on her work, on her classes, on teaching thirty teenage boys about the Victorian class system and the concept of nobility. Was it in the blood? Was it earned? Or was the entire idea of the "gentleman" a farce?

Friday came around and Gwen delivered her final lectures and led her last discussions on *Great Expectations*. Not only had the boys finished the book in under a week, they had enjoyed it, they said. They only wished Dickens hadn't written two endings. They had no idea which one to consider the "real" ending—the quiet philosophical one or the happier one where Pip ran off with an older and wiser Estella?

Gwen only saw Edwin a few times all week, always during dinner in the dining hall with all the boys present. Thank goodness she had Mr. Price and Mr. Reynolds to talk to or she might have packed her bags and left earlier.

Or would she have? As much as Edwin had hurt her, the students had healed her. Teaching them was such a pleasure, it hardly felt like work. Their questions surprised her, made her think.

As boys about Pip's age, they had their own take on his motivations that were different from her adult woman's perspective. She learned as much from them as they learned from her.

At the end of each class on Friday, she thanked all the boys for giving her such a wonderful week at William Marshal Academy. She said she wasn't sure if she'd be back next week as that was the headmaster's decision. But whatever happened, she would treasure her week among them as one of the best of her life.

"If he doesn't hire you," Laird said, "we're all quitting school."

"Be sure to tell him that," Gwen replied with a wink.

The boys filed out of the room. Gwen sat at her desk for a long time before working up the courage to exit. She didn't want to leave Marshal. She didn't want to stay, either. Not after what happened with Edwin and that terrible, wonderful kiss.

The ball was in his court. If he wanted her to stay, she would stay...but she was not going to remain somewhere she wasn't welcome.

Gwen went for another walk that afternoon, this time in search of the apple trees Laird had assured her were behind the school grounds. Sure enough, a rusty-hinged wooden door out back led her into a wild apple orchard.

She gazed out at the patch of apple trees, at their bent and bowed limbs hanging heavy with red September apples. Reaching out, she plucked an apple from the nearest tree and took a bite. The tartness of it set her teeth on edge. The juice wet her fingers. Her mouth burst with the bright flavor.

She wanted to stay.

There and then she decided it. Life was here. Learning was here. Whether or not she and Edwin would work out their differences...it didn't matter. Laird was sweet, but he was also wrong. Eve didn't need Adam as long as she had her apples.

Gwen stepped onto the dirt path behind the school, but she paused when she saw two figures moving through the trees, not far from her. One she recognized immediately—Christopher, Laird's best friend and partner in rogue welcoming committee activities. He was walking alongside an old man who had to be in his seventies or eighties. Despite the age difference between them, Gwen thought she could detect a family resemblance. They were nearly the same height and walked with a similar long-legged gait. Both of them held their shoulders a certain tense way. Was this Christopher's grandfather, come to visit him?

They were headed her direction, but neither seemed to see her yet through the trees. They were walking side-by-side in total silence.

Actually, that wasn't quite right. The old man appeared to be crying—small sobs, but sobs nonetheless.

The old man paused less than ten yards from her. Christopher stopped, too, but made no effort to console him. She watched as the old man laid a hand on the nearest tree and brought a handkerchief to his face. No, not a handkerchief. A white napkin. A white napkin with a red border. He must have been to the same diner in town where Gwen had stopped for coffee.

Gwen wanted to announce herself, but couldn't find the courage to interrupt such an emotional moment. She watched, rooted in place, as the man regained control of himself. He stood up straight and continued past her without looking in her direction. Christopher, trailing behind him, met her eyes. He threw her a sheepish smile as if embarrassed by his grandfather's display of emotion.

For a few days now, Gwen had almost convinced herself she was living in a long-gone time. It certainly seemed that way out here in the foothills on most days.

But the old man climbed into a late-model Lexus and, without so much as a wave to his grandson, drove off.

Christopher watched as the car disappeared down the path back to civilization. Gwen squeezed his shoulder to show she understood. He didn't try to shrug her off, but he didn't offer any explanation. Families were complicated, which she understood all too well from her own limited experience.

Gwen returned to her cottage. As she swung open the door, she found Edwin waiting for her in her drawing room.

CHAPTER EIGHT

Gwen could only marvel at the sight of the headmaster for a moment. She would have been less surprised to find the Bride dancing the samba in her parlor than she was at the sight of Edwin standing there.

"I'm sorry," she finally said after recovering. "I don't recall you knocking on my door."

"For the record, I did knock. I'm not to be blamed that you weren't around to hear it," Edwin said.

"So you just let yourself in?"

"Yes."

"That's breaking and entering."

"I broke nothing," he said. "So it's merely entering."

Gwen pursed her lips at him. "Are you here to fire me?"

"I can't fire you as I haven't hired you," he said, his hands still in his jacket pockets. He seemed to be attempting to look casual and comfortable. Instead, he looked tense and worried.

"I did good work with the boys this week," she said, crossing her arms. "I just want you to know that. We had great discussions. And they wrote fantastic essays on what it means to be gentlemen. You should read them. You might learn something."

Edwin's eyes flashed again. Then he sighed and nodded. "I owe you an explanation, Miss Ashby."

"Yes, for a lot of things," she agreed and sat down on the sofa. "For starters, why haven't you spoken to me since our dinner?"

He picked up one of the wooden chairs and moved it in front of where she was perched nervously on the edge of the sofa cushion.

"Monday night," he said, sitting down and facing her. "No—I'm starting in the wrong place. Forgive me, Miss Ashby."

"Didn't we have this discussion? You can call me Gwen. Or Gwendolyn if that's just too casual for your liking."

"I do like Gwendolyn."

"My grandparents always called me Gwendolyn. I liked it when they did."

"And when I do it?" he asked, a hint of uncertainty in his voice. Usually he sounded so sure of himself, so stolid and sturdy.

A small hairline crack formed in her anger at the sound of his nervousness. "I like it when you do, too," she admitted.

"Very good then, Gwendolyn," he said. "I'm not quite

sure where to start. Miss Muir left us so suddenly, and I admitted Samuel to the school... Things have been complicated ever since. Complicated enough that I don't feel comfortable bringing in an outsider to our *unique* situation."

"Unique? You pissed off some parents. Students left. Now you're rebuilding the teaching staff and the student body. Lots of schools go through this, Edwin."

"No school has ever gone through what ours has gone through. Not entirely. I'm certain of that. And there would be consequences—serious consequences—if I let you stay. Though I admit the final say isn't mine." He paused. "It's yours."

"You need a new literature teacher. Or are you planning on teaching *Ivanhoe* for eternity?"

"Eternity," he repeated, then laughed softly to himself. "No, I didn't mean there would be consequences to letting a teacher into the school. Although there would be. What I meant...what I mean is...Gwendolyn, if I let you in..."

Edwin looked at her with imploring eyes and a hand over his heart. Now she understood. He didn't mean there would be consequences to letting her into the school. No, he meant there would be consequences to letting her into his heart.

She reached out and took his hand in hers. "Edwin..."

He looked down at their clasped hands as if he'd never seen such a thing before—a woman taking a man's hand in her own.

"It's not in my nature to have casual dalliances," he said. "I have never had casual dalliances. It's not the gentleman's way to play with a woman's affections without honorable intentions."

"Honorable intentions?" Gwen repeated, utterly incredulous. "You mean if we become lovers, you'll want us to get married?"

"I believe that is the definition of honorable intentions."

"Are you really religious or something?"

Edwin furrowed his brow. "I was christened and raised in the Church of England. Of course I'm not religious."

Gwen pondered that a moment. The pondering turned into a laugh.

"You are living in the wrong time," she said, squeezing Edwin's hand. "You should have been born in the Regency era. You would have made a wonderful Mr. Darcy."

"I take that as a compliment," he said, a smile at last playing across his lips. "Fitzwilliam Darcy, although briefly blinded by prejudice against Miss Bennett's family situation, allowed his better instincts to win the day. He knew a marriage of true minds and good hearts was vastly superior to a union born out of pure duty to his station in life."

"I also think Elizabeth Bennet and Fitzwilliam Darcy wanted to rip each other's clothes off."

"I believe you're reading a great deal of subtext into the work."

"I love the subtext," she said. "I told you the boys wrote essays this week on what it means to be gentlemen. You want to know what I think a gentleman is?"

"I believe you're going to tell me whether I want you to or not."

"I am," she said, putting her hand back in her lap. "I think a gentleman respects women, and doesn't pretend to know better than his lady what is good or bad for her. I think a gentleman is brave enough to eschew the silly rules society tries to enforce on women. I think a gentleman tells the world to mind its own business and concerns himself only with what he and the lady in his life want to do together in private."

"You have an interesting definition of a gentleman."

"It's admittedly a little self-serving. Then again...that was the most amazing kiss of my life, Edwin."

He exhaled heavily, a little shudder in his breath.

She knew how he felt. Her lips still tingled with the memory of that incredible kiss.

"I'm pleased to hear it affected you as much as it affected me," he said. "I haven't stopped thinking about it since Monday evening. Gwendolyn, you must understand that it's not in my nature to behave rakishly with you. I respect you far too much."

"Then respect me enough to trust that I'm old enough and wise enough to decide to be with you and to live with the consequences. I'm twenty-five years old, Edwin. I'm not a virgin. I'm on birth control. I'm an adult. Please treat me accordingly."

Edwin raised his hand and caressed her cheek. "If only it were that simple," he said, lowering his hand.

Gwen saw something in his eyes, a look she didn't quite understand but desperately wanted to. It wasn't shyness so much as reticence. He had a secret he wanted to tell her but didn't know how.

"Your wife was the only woman you've ever been with, wasn't she?"

"A gentleman should not discuss such personal matters with a lady."

"What if that lady is his lover?"

"Then that's a different matter entirely," he said.

"How long has it been since you've been with someone?"

"A very long time," he confessed almost sheepishly.

"Then you should come upstairs and make love to me," she said, taking his hand in hers and guiding it to her thigh. "The lady insists."

"You insist, you say?"

"Yes, and it would be rude of you to say no to such a humble request."

"It would, wouldn't it?"

"Quite," Gwen said as Edwin slid his hand up her thigh. She shivered from the heat of his touch.

"Ungentlemanly, even," he said.

"First, do I have the job?" she asked. "We should probably decide that now. Might not be a good idea to make a hiring decision in bed."

"Thirteen boys stood in my office today to tell me they would mutiny if you weren't hired."

"Only thirteen?" she teased.

"That's all that could fit in my office. The rest stood in the hallway."

"I never want to leave this place," Gwen said, looking into his dark green eyes.

"If you truly feel that way, then you'll never have to. Now that that's out of the way…"

Their lips met again, and just like the first time they kissed, Gwen felt a shock of electricity traveling through her entire body. She'd never known desire like what she felt for Edwin.

He seemed equally enamored of her. She quickly found herself on his lap, his arms around her as his mouth poured kisses onto her lips. She pushed Edwin's jacket down his arms as he assaulted her neck with bites and licks. The heat from his tongue penetrated her skin. As soon as his jacket was off, he lifted her up with shockingly strong arms. He carried her up the stairs to the bedroom and laid her carefully on the soft white sheets. She sat up and unbuttoned his vest while he kissed her again. She ran her hands up and down his firm chest under the silky cotton of his perfectly pressed shirt.

As much as she wanted to tear Edwin's clothes off, she held back and let him take the lead. She wanted him to take the lead, wanted him to do whatever he wished to her as hard and as often as he wished to do it. For all his earlier apprehension, he now seemed entirely collected, in charge, and determined to make love to her.

His mouth traced a path from her lips to the center of her chest. He gently pushed her onto her back and unbuttoned her blouse with adroit and purposeful fingers. She couldn't wait to be naked for him. Such a man deserved to have a woman in his bed giving him pleasure every single night of his life. She wanted to be that woman.

Edwin kissed the tops of her breasts as his fingers caressed the lacy edges of her bra. For what felt like eons, he gently tortured her with his mouth and his hands, touching every part of her except the parts that most wished to be touched. She thought he was teasing her at first by making her wait so long, but then she realized he was simply being gentlemanly even now.

"Edwin," she whispered, laying a hand on his cheek. She felt the slightest hint of stubble on his face, so sturdy and masculine. "I want you. You don't have to be afraid to do to me anything and everything you want to do."

"You say that now," he said with a roguish smile.

She smiled back. "I'll say it after, too. Promise."

Her words had the desired effect. Edwin pushed her skirt up all the way to her stomach. He wrenched her panties down her legs and tossed them onto the floor. She opened her legs for him, eager for him to see her. With one hand he loosened his tie and pulled it off. With his other hand, he pressed one and then two fingers into her wetness. She gasped at the first penetration. Pleasure exploded from the core of her, reverberating through her entire body as he touched her inside.

"More," she begged, and he pulled his fingers out of her and opened his pants. She couldn't get him inside her fast enough. He parted her inner lips with his fingers, spreading her open. She felt the tip at the entrance of her body. Slowly, he pushed into her. The pleasure of his thick cock was beyond anything she could have imagined. He embedded himself deep in her with one quick hard thrust, and Gwen gasped his name.

He covered her mouth with his hand and Gwen froze. Then she heard the sound of boys' voices just outside her cottage.

Edwin smiled down at her and whispered a quiet, "Shhh...."

She nodded, and he started to move inside her with long, slow strokes, his hand still over her mouth. She didn't mind it. She loved his forcefulness, his control of her and his own body. They were still clothed, both of them. Only the parts of them joined together were naked. But she loved this, loved feeling sealed to him, naked hip to naked hip.

Slowly, he let his hand slide from her mouth down her neck. Gwen struggled to keep herself silent. It was torture not to sigh, not to moan as Edwin pulled the strap of her lacy bra down her arm and bared her right breast. He latched onto it and sucked, his tongue swirling around her nipple. She was burning, burning alive from the touch of his hands on her, his mouth on her breast, his length filling her up more than any man ever had in her life.

She pushed her hips up against him. The pleasure was building up in her like a bullet in a chamber desperate to fire. She would die underneath him if she didn't come soon.

They made love in near-total silence. Only a few hushed grunts and gasps escaped their throats. The silence intensified the pleasure as she had to hold everything inside when all she wanted to do was moan and let it all out. They felt like conspirators, she and Edwin, as they moved together in necessary silence. She clutched at his shoulders and wrapped her legs over the back of his thighs. He teased her nipples again and again while pushing the hardness of him inside her with slow, brutal thrusts.

His mouth found hers once more and she kissed him hungrily. Yes, she wanted this forever, wanted to give him this pleasure until the end of time, wanted to be the woman in his bed who spread her legs for him, welcomed him inside her, and gave him a safe place to be the powerful, strong, erotic man he was born to be.

His hands scored her back as the speed of his thrusts increased. She felt the pounding in the pit of her stomach, felt her inner muscles tensing around him. Wetness poured out of her onto the bedsheet. Never had she felt so wanton or so primal in her life. It was as if this man were more than human, and he made her something more as well simply by entering her body with his.

He placed his hands on either side of her shoulders and pushed himself up so that their hips alone met. She lay beneath him, a being of surrender and submission. She closed her eyes and lost herself in his thrusts. The need mounted in her; the knot in her stomach tightened...

When she came, it was with his hand once again over her mouth to stifle her gasps. Her shoulders flinched off the bed as her climax burst through her, every muscle inside her furiously fluttering around him. Once she'd ridden out her own orgasm, he finally let himself erupt. He looked down at her and met her eyes for one perfect moment before shutting them tight. His entire body went still as he came inside her, filling her with his heat.

Gwen wrapped her arms and legs around him as he collapsed on top of her. She couldn't get enough of the warmth of his body and the feel of his rapidly racing heart against her naked chest.

He kissed her as he pulled out of her.

"Now that," she whispered, "was very gentlemanly."

CHAPTER NINE

For a few beautiful minutes, Gwen lay in Edwin's arms doing nothing but breathing and relishing the way her body reverberated with the aftershocks of sex.

"I can't stay in your bed tonight," he whispered. "I have to set a good example for the boys."

"If those boys grow up to be half as good in bed as you are, then their future wives and girlfriends will owe you a debt of gratitude," she said. "Or boyfriends."

"Don't even mention wives and girlfriends to those boys. They already beg me to let girls into the school enough as it is. No matter how often I tell them the school's charter specifically states the endowment will be revoked—"

"Now that does sound terrible. I'd never want your endowments revoked." Gwen curled up on Edwin's chest and gave him a wink.

"I'll revoke my endowment if you don't behave your-self, young lady."

Gwen only laughed. How beautiful to see Edwin so relaxed, so at peace. Tomorrow they would return to pretending they disliked each other, but tonight there was no hiding. He wanted her as much as she wanted him.

"Speaking of endowment, do I not get to see you naked?" she teased. He'd already straightened his clothes and combed his fingers through his hair. Her disheveled appearance and his wetness inside her were the only proof that, just minutes before, Edwin had been buried inside her and thrusting wildly. She adored both Edwins —the civilized headmaster and the primal lover. But tonight she wanted the lover, not the headmaster.

"See me naked? Miss Ashby, I have to wonder if you've ever seen an unclothed man before. We aren't nearly as aesthetically pleasing as women."

"I beg to differ. I'd far rather see you naked than see myself naked. I see myself naked all the time."

"Then I envy you."

"Would you like to see me naked?" she asked. She still had her skirt on, her shoes, her bra that she'd pulled back up. Even her blouse was still on if unbuttoned.

"Without a doubt. But there will be time for that."

"Is now the time?" she asked, tossing her shirt aside.

He kissed her and smiled. "No. But soon. Alas, duty calls. It's Friday evening, my turn to monitor the dining hall."

Gwen glanced at the clock on the wall—6:30. Dinner

every night was served at seven o'clock on the dot. She'd asked two days ago who did all the cooking, and she'd been stunned to learn the boys cooked their own meals. It was an innovation Edwin had implemented. The students needed to learn basic culinary skills. A man should not rely on his wife or mother to take care of him his whole life. The boys might join the military or delay marriage for years to finish their schooling. Knowing how to take care of themselves was part of being a true gentleman. Also, it fostered a sense of community, Mr. Price had told her. The boys served each other, learned to plan, learned team-work. And no one had gotten food poisoning yet. Still, a kitchen full of teenage boys could turn to chaos in an instant. Adult supervision was a moral imperative. It would be Gwen's turn soon.

"I can't keep you from your duty," Gwen said as Edwin pulled away from her arms. He picked his vest up and pulled it on. "Or keep you from dinner."

"Rest assured, I'll be doing everything in my power not to think of you the entire time," she said.

"That's fine. I'll be here in bed thinking of you making love to me enough for both of us." She laid back on the pillows and stretched out, luxuriating on the sheets. She unhooked her bra behind her back and started to pull it off.

"I'm suddenly reminded why I dislike you so much, Miss Ashby. You're vicious."

"You're luscious."

"I'm leaving is what I am," Edwin said before kissing her one more time. "You can't be trusted."

"I know. I'm awful, aren't I?" she asked as Edwin tried and failed twice to knot his tie. She dropped her bra on the floor and knelt in front of him. Naked from the waist up, she took his tie and pressed her breasts against his chest. "Absolutely horrible."

"And unrepentant, as well," Edwin said, narrowing his eyes at her.

She tied his tie for him even as his left hand sneaked up to caress her breast. He'd been in her just moments ago, but she already wanted him inside her again.

"Entirely," she said. "Have a good dinner, Headmaster Yorke. I'll stay in tonight. If I go to the dining hall with you, I might do something terrible—like kiss you in front of the boys." She kissed him on the mouth, and he kissed her back with undisguised need.

"You wouldn't dare."

"Try me," she said.

"I'm glad I hired you," Edwin said from the door. "Now I can fire you."

"Fire me all you want. I'm not going anywhere."

"I was afraid of that," he said, leaving her alone on the bed. She listened to his footsteps on the stairs. He would find his jacket in the living room. No doubt he was now paused by the mirror, checking his appearance for any telltale signs he'd been engaging in ungentlemanly behavior with one of his teachers only moments earlier. At last, she heard the door to her cottage open and close. He was gone.

Feeling weightless and lazy, Gwen did nothing but lie back in bed and bask in the afterglow. Her body still buzzed with memories of Edwin, memories she wanted to hang onto forever. But as much as she tried to focus on the physical pleasure he'd just given her, she couldn't stop herself from dreaming of a future with him. She adored him. No question. She couldn't deny it even if she wanted to. Chance had brought her to this school—a random stop at a diner, and here she was, literature teacher at the prestigious William Marshal Academy and lover of the headmaster.

Lover... She loved being his lover. But was it just that? Was there more? Gwen knew she wanted to stay at this school for the rest of her life. But was it because of the school? The students? Or the headmaster?

If this had been a multiple-choice test, she knew what she would have answered.

All of the above.

With reluctance she felt in her whole body, Gwen rose and walked to the bathroom. She'd expected to feel sore after such intense lovemaking—Edwin had held nothing back, clearly—but she'd never felt better. She started a bath, for no other reason than to feel the water surround her naked body and imagine Edwin's arms around her again.

She lay back in the hot water, washing her hair, her body. She traced the path of Edwin's kisses on her mouth, neck, and breasts with her fingers...

She stayed in the water until it went cool before getting out. *It's Friday night*, she thought, toweling off. *Barely nine o'clock, and I'm ready for bed.*

Gwen had never gotten to bed this early in her entire academic career. Before she came here, she stayed up well past midnight working, answering emails, and writing papers with the hopes of getting published in scholarly journals. But that part of her life was gone now. Poof. No more emails. No more late-night writing binges. No more "publish or perish." All that madness was gone, and she didn't miss it. Had the quiet life of a boarding school teacher been what she'd wanted all along?

Looking back, she must have known her relationship with Cary was going nowhere. She'd thrown herself into the academic rat race even though she resented how far it took her from her real passion—teaching. But that was all over now. As of today, she was the new literature teacher at the William Marshal Academy. Edwin hadn't asked for her CV, or if she was published in the *New England Journal of American Literature*. Her only responsibility going forward was to teach thirty boys everything she knew about literature. And, of course, to take care of Edwin's every sexual want, need, and desire. Not exactly a job requirement, no, but she considered that aspect one of the fringe benefits.

So she could go to bed early if she wanted, right? Nothing else to do. She'd taught her classes, gone on a walk, had sex with the headmaster, had her bath. A full day, and now it was over...but it didn't have to be. A light was flickering behind the stained glass on the fifth floor of the main building. Edwin was back in the headmaster's residence, still up.

She studied the courtyard from her window and saw no one out and about. The evening had promised to turn cold, and it had kept its promise. All the boys were inside their dorms.

Gwen changed from her flannel pajamas into her clothes from earlier. If someone caught her, she would at least look semi-professional.

Carefully and quietly, she slipped out of her cottage and walked briskly toward the main building. She kept her head high and her face forward. She didn't want to look like she was sneaking around after dark...even though that was exactly what she was doing. In the off-chance she bumped into Mr. Reynolds or Mr. Price, she had a half-dozen excellent and valid reasons for going to the headmaster's quarters, things she had been planning to bring to Edwin's attention anyway. Mentally, Gwen ran through the list:

1. She'd found Miss Muir's family Bible. She really should mail that to her. Perhaps the headmaster had her address.
2. She needed to get laid. Again.
3. What sort of grading scale did they employ at William Marshal?
4. Did she already mention needing to get laid again?

She reached the main building with a sigh of relief. She went up all five flights and knocked on Edwin's door. After an interminable pause, he answered it. He'd taken off his jacket and vest, but hadn't undone his tie yet. She would have to help him with that.

"Miss Ashby, I hope you have a valid reason for knocking on my door this late at night," he said. His voice was stern but his eyes were playful.

"Yes. Many valid reasons. At least two. And one invalid reason."

"And the invalid reason?"

She rose on her tiptoes and kissed him.

Gwen had expected some chiding, some pushback, some playing hard to get from him as punishment for visiting him so soon after their tryst. Instead, she got his tongue in her mouth, which is exactly where she wanted it. He pulled her inside and kicked the door shut behind them so hard she heard the paintings on the wall rattle in their frames.

She began unbuttoning his shirt as he ran his hands up and down her back. "I missed your bedroom all week," she said, her voice breathless. "I was only in it a couple of hours, I believe."

"How long would you like to be in it tonight?"

"Oh, until next Friday at the very least."

Taking her by the hand, Edwin pulled her through the living room and into the bedroom. He shut the door behind them and loosened his tie. Now with two doors between them and campus, she could be as loud as she wanted. Good. She wanted him to hear how much he pleased her. She wanted to hear him say her name when inside her.

He kissed her neck hungrily as she pulled his shirt out from his pants, brushing his hardness. Soon his shirt (and hers) were on the floor, Edwin's tie dangling undone around his neck. He was muscular and lean, and she wanted to bite that little vein that pulsed in his biceps. With unconcealed pleasure, she kissed his bare chest and ran her hands over his rib cage.

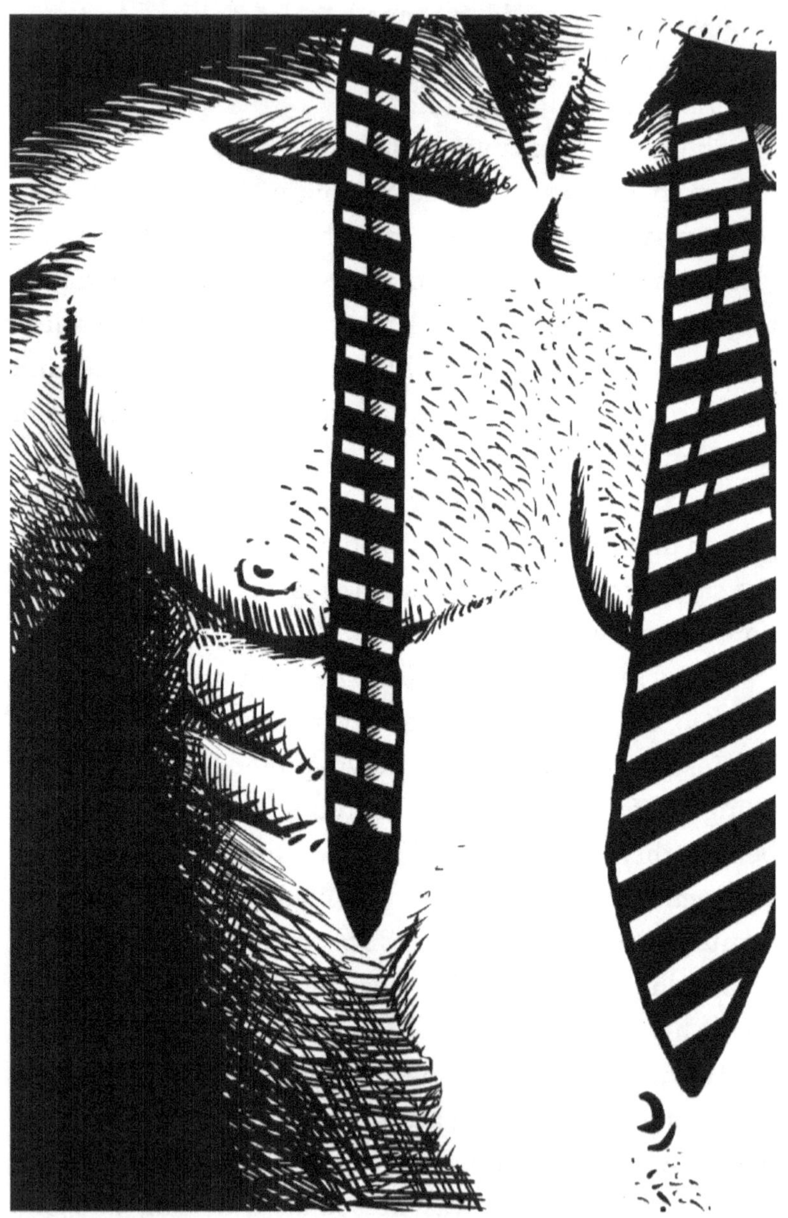

*He was muscular and lean, and she wanted to bite that
little vein that pulsed in his biceps.*

She started in on his belt, but he pushed her hands aside. He unzipped her skirt and pushed it all the way down, leaving her in nothing but her white silk slip. She hadn't bothered with panties or a bra. They just would have gotten in the way. This time, she wanted nothing between her body and Edwin's.

She slipped out of his arms and backed up to the bedpost. Slowly, seductively, she pushed the straps of her slip down her arms, pushed the fabric over her breasts, and let it fall to the floor. Now she was naked, except for her shoes (which didn't really count). He was so tall that she had decided to keep her shoes on until he'd gotten her horizontal.

"Your turn," she said.

Edwin unbuckled his black leather belt and slid it off. Her breath caught in her throat at the sight of the leather strap in his large hands. Maybe some night she'd talk him into playing a game of Stern Headmaster Punishes the Naughty Student.

"You're exquisite, Gwendolyn," he said, unbuttoning his pants. "Beyond beautiful. If I could sculpt, I'd make a career out of capturing your curves in marble for posterity."

"You already have me here naked. You don't have to sweet-talk me."

"It's simply the truth," he said. "And a gentleman tells the truth."

He'd kicked his slippers off—had he been wearing those since answering the door?—and then stepped out of his pants and dark silk boxer shorts.

"Speaking of sculpting someone out of marble," she said, stepping forward and wrapping her hand around his hard length, "marble would not do a body like yours justice."

He closed his eyes as she stroked him. "Gwendolyn, let me touch you…"

Gwen covered his lips with her finger. "You take care of this entire school," she said. "Let me take care of you."

She dropped to her knees in front of him. Edwin gasped as she kissed the tip of him with her tongue.

"Gwendolyn…" he said again, in obvious shock.

"Just enjoy it, Edwin," she ordered. "Even ladies give gentlemen blow jobs."

"Are you certain of that?"

"Absolutely. And I promise, this will be a ladylike blow job."

With all her heart, she wanted to give him the most pleasure he'd experienced in his life. She took him in her mouth and caressed him with her tongue. She ran her hands over his hard thighs as she sucked him, gently scratching the delicate skin of his hips and stomach. He gasped and flinched, and she rejoiced at knowing that he was enjoying what she was doing to him. He might have even been enjoying receiving her attentions as much as she was enjoying giving them.

"Gwendolyn…" he breathed. She tasted the first drops of salt on her tongue. "I need to be inside you."

She let him pull out of her mouth. Still on her knees, she smiled up at him. "If you insist."

"I do insist," he said, taking her by the arm and

pulling her to her feet. He captured her mouth with a kiss, which he abruptly broke off.

"What is it?" she asked.

"I can taste myself on your lips." He seemed surprised. Not at all bothered. Simply surprised.

"You've never tasted yourself on a woman's mouth before?"

He shook his head. "Never."

"You poor man."

He laughed and kissed her again with renewed passion. As he kissed her, he eased her onto her back on the scarlet sheets. She wasted no time, opening her legs for him.

The only light in the room came from the antique table lamp on the bedside table. But it was enough to illuminate every part of his beautiful body. He was looking at her with such desire that she could barely breathe. His eyes were filled with need, his lips parted and panting.

Edwin went down on her, feasting on her with his mouth and fingers. His tongue found her clitoris, and his fingers pushed into that soft spot just inside her that made every muscle in her body tense when touched.

"There," she said, grasping his forearm with her hand. "Right there. Like that."

He'd found the perfect tempo, the perfect rhythm. Everything went tight inside her. Tight and tighter. She held onto his arm with a death grip as every breath brought her closer and closer and pushed her higher and higher, and just when she couldn't take it anymore, she came with a rush and a shudder that shook her to her core.

She barely had time to recover from her orgasm when Edwin pulled her off the bed and back to her feet. He kissed her, and this time she could taste herself on him. Before she could kick off her shoes, he turned her around and placed her hands on the bedpost. She started to ask what he was doing, but then he entered her from behind, her wet body giving him no resistance.

Gwen rested her forehead on the back of her hands and gasped with every one of his rough thrusts. She turned her head to the side and saw their reflections in the cheval mirror.

Had she seen anything so beautiful in her life as the sight of her body joined with Edwin's? She watched, mesmerized, as he moved in and out of her, his erection slick with her wetness. His right hand held her by the hip, held her steady as he thrust into her. His left hand roamed the front of her body, cupping her breast and plucking her nipple. Her second climax built as his thrusts went on and on. She'd never been with a man of such stamina before.

"You can come whenever you want," she said between ragged breaths. "You don't have to wait for me."

"Ladies first," he said, and Gwen laughed.

She took his left hand and guided it between her legs. She showed him where to touch her, how to touch her. He took instruction beautifully. He massaged the tight knot of flesh between his fingers until Gwen cried out with her second climax. She stood limp and spent as Edwin held her by her waist and thrust up and into her. He came in near silence, the only sound a soft exhalation. She shivered as she felt the heat of his breath on her naked back.

She leaned back against his chest, and he wrapped his

arms around her. He had such magnificent forearms. Sinewy and muscular. The fingernail marks she'd left in them only added to their appeal.

"I want to sleep in your bed tonight," she said. "Can I do that?"

Edwin turned her to face him, and she wound her arms around his neck. Good thing she had kept her two-inch heels on the whole time. Made it a little easier to kiss him.

"It would hardly be gentlemanly to send you out in the cold dark night all alone," he said.

"Yes, those fifty yards between Hawkwood Hall and my cottage could be deadly."

"You never know what ill could befall you," Edwin said, running his fingers through her hair. "Bears. Snakes."

"Lions. Tigers."

"Fires," he said.

"I don't know. I think all the fire is right..." She kissed his chest. "...here."

Edwin pulled the covers down and they both slid into bed. She stretched out on top of him and rested her head on his chest.

"Now that we're lovers, are you going to tell me all those personal matters you said you couldn't discuss with a lady?" she asked.

"No," he said.

"No? Did you say no?"

"Was 'no' the incorrect response?" he asked.

"It was the opposite of the correct response," she said. "You said those personal matters of your past would be inappropriate to discuss with a lady. I said, 'What if that lady was your lover and you were in bed together?'"

"And if I don't tell you?"

"I guess we'd no longer be lovers then."

"Well," he said with a sigh. "When you put it that way..."

CHAPTER TEN

"My past is not terribly interesting," Edwin began once they'd settled into his bed. Such a luxuriously comfortable bed, Gwen could spend the rest of her life inside it. She hoped Edwin felt the same way about her body.

"Stop stalling," she ordered, and Edwin sighed heavily. She laughed as his chest moved under her cheek with the force of that sigh. "Everything about you is interesting. You're an Englishman with an overdeveloped sense of duty and chivalry running an all-boys boarding school in the shadow of the Appalachian Mountains. I can't begin to guess how that happened."

"It's really quite simple. After the war—"

"War?" Gwen said, heart skipping. "You were in the war?"

"Yes, but not for long. It ended a year after I was commissioned. I didn't see combat."

"You were an officer?"

"Low level," he said with a wave of his hand.

She sat up so she could glower at him. "This is a British thing, isn't it? Not telling people anything about your life?"

"Is it in an 'American thing' to pry?"

She glared at him. "Sarcasm must also be a British thing."

"I merely asked," he said, though she could see him valiantly battling the urge to smile.

"I've never met a more British man in my life," she said, resting her head back on his chest.

"Thank you," he said.

"It wasn't a compliment. Go on."

"After the war, I went to university. I enjoyed what little taste of authority I had experienced in the army. I thought leading a classroom of children would be a similar sort of challenge and reward."

Gwen did the math in her head. She wasn't sure of Edwin's age, but she guessed he was about forty. The Gulf War ended in 1991, which meant Edwin was barely twenty when he was in the army. Just a boy not much older than the ones at William Marshal.

"My parents' closest friends were a wealthy couple who'd helped them through some difficult times, especially when I was in the army. They had a daughter a few years younger than me. It was our parents' dearest wish that she and I would marry. I adored my parents and couldn't bear to disappoint them."

"You married out of duty to your parents?" she asked, utterly incredulous. "Not even Mr. Darcy did that."

"Mr. Darcy's parents were dead."

"Right," she said. "Good point."

"Victoria was an attractive girl, intelligent and kind so I hardly considered it a sacrifice. We weren't in love, but we respected each other and had a solid friendship. The first few weeks of our marriage, however, were...difficult."

"Had you been with anyone before her?" she asked.

"Yes."

Gwen drummed her fingers on his chest. He said nothing. She drummed harder.

"Gwendolyn? Are you attempting to beat me to death with your fingers? I can suggest some more efficient killing techniques if you are."

She sat up again and looked down at him. "Who were you with before you were with your wife? It better be the queen or there's no excuse for being so secretive."

"It wasn't the queen, I'm afraid. She was the widowed mother of one of my schoolmates. Before you're too terribly scandalized, I was eighteen and she was only thirty-six."

"I'm not scandalized at all. What happened with you and your friend's mom?"

"He was away and asked me to check on his mother who had no other children. I won't say she seduced me, but I promise I went to her home only to see if I could be of service to her."

"And then you were of service to her," Gwen teased.

"I was of service to her three times the first night alone," Edwin said, then laughed. "Our rather meaning-less affair lasted for the summer."

"Did she teach you all sorts of sexy things? The ways of women and all that?"

"She was instructive, yes. But hardly affectionate. Things were...perfunctory between us."

"Perfunctory? That might be the least sexy description of sex I've ever heard," Gwen said.

"Perfunctory but thorough."

"If it was that thorough, she would have gone down on you."

"She did."

"But you said you'd never tasted yourself on a woman's lips before..."

"That's because she never kissed me."

"Never after, or..."

"Never *never*," he said. "She said we weren't to have that sort of relationship. Feelings would complicate things more than they already were." Edwin spoke the words with little emotion, but Gwen heard the ghost of hurt pride hiding behind the dispassionate tone.

She leaned over, took Edwin's face in her hands, and kissed him. She kissed him like he deserved to be kissed, like he should have been kissed the night he lost his virginity and every night thereafter. She kissed him so long and so hard that she almost forgot why she started kissing him in the first place other than kissing him was the best idea she'd ever had. He kissed back with his hands on her naked shoulders and his chest warm against her breasts.

"What was that for?" Edwin asked when Gwen finally pulled back.

"An apology kiss on behalf of all womankind."

"Apology accepted."

"Now go on with your story," she said as she straddled his hips and rested on top of him again.

"My first lover, as I said, was thorough if indifferent. I felt confident I would be able to please my new bride once we were married. I was sadly mistaken, however."

"The first few times can really hurt for a woman. I was in pain about the first two weeks after I started having sex."

"It wasn't physical pain," Edwin said, caressing her back with his fingertips. "I could tell my wife had already been with someone. I didn't mind. I had, as well. But she cried when we tried—before and after. I offered to stop and wait for a few weeks. Months would pass between attempts. After a year of feigning happiness in public and awkwardness in private, I discovered the cause of our incompatibility. Victoria had another lover."

"God, that must have been devastating." Gwen kissed his chest in sympathy.

"It was a shock, to say the least. I hadn't even suspected. But then by accident, I came home a day early from a trip and discovered her in bed with her lover. She confessed to everything."

"Were you angry?"

"No," he said.

Gwen believed him. "I would have been furious," she said. "I would have been tempted to beat the hell out of that man."

"But you see," Edwin sighed, "it wasn't a man."

Gwen rolled up and stared down at Edwin in wide-eyed surprise. "Your wife was gay?"

"Gay?"

"You know, a lesbian? Played for the other team? A member of the Sapphic sisterhood?"

"She was, yes," he said after a pause. "She'd secretly been involved with a female 'friend' of hers for years. The marriage to me was meant to shield their relationship from scrutiny. My kindness to her, she said, made things more unbearable. She hated that she had trapped me in a loveless marriage. There was nothing else to do. We divorced on grounds of adultery."

"Well, at least she took responsibility."

"She didn't, Gwendolyn. Her parents would have disowned her had the truth come out. I allowed Victoria to claim I had strayed."

Gwen's heart twisted, her blood quickened, her smile fell. "You... I just have no words for you."

"It was the only thing a gentleman could do. My family was, of course, furious and ashamed. I'd brought embarrassment onto their good name with the divorce. I packed my things and came to America. I found work here at the William Marshal Academy, and when the headmaster retired, I was elevated to his position." He paused. "I told you it wasn't an interesting story."

"You were seduced by a friend's mother, served in wartime as an officer, and were married to a lesbian and divorced all by age...?"

"Twenty-four," he said.

"If that's not an interesting story then I don't know what is."

"I'm sure your life story is far more interesting than mine."

"It isn't at all." Gwen pulled a pillow to her chest. "I

was born in Asheville. Grew up among the hippies and hipsters. Normal childhood. Loved reading. Bit of a nerd. Like I told you, both my parents are gone."

"Gwendolyn...I'm so sorry."

"Orphan by age eighteen. I guess it does sound Dickensian, doesn't it? But I never became a street urchin."

"How did you cope with losing both your parents?"

"It was hard," she confessed. "But books saved me. I know that sounds silly and glib. But I lost myself in books. Read constantly. I was a glutton for fiction. Any world was better than my own. Elizabeth Bennet had a fool for a mother, but better a living crazy mom than a dead one. And then Mr. Darcy came along and saw her virtues, plucked her from obscurity, and made her his wife. Perfect. I wanted a Mr. Darcy of my own. And Jane Eyre, she was an orphan like me. And yet so much braver and stronger than I ever hoped to be." She sighed. "Being alone in Asheville wasn't much fun so I moved to New Orleans—in my head, that is—and lived with some fictional vampires for a while. Vampires, wizards... I got into more serious reading in college. Faulkner. Flannery O'Connor."

"Faulkner? Modern tripe."

"Oh, hush. Not every book has to be *Ivanhoe*. Anyway, my grandparents accused me of hiding in my books. But I wasn't hiding. I was healing. Those stories made me believe bad things happened for a reason and good things happened if you kept going all the way to the end. Hope and perseverance—that's what I learned from books. So now I teach literature to teenage boys. Maybe they'll learn some hope and perseverance, too."

"Was your hope and perseverance rewarded?" Edwin asked, his voice soft.

Gwen smiled. "I'm a teacher at the world's weirdest school—the William Marshal Academy," she said. "And I'm in your bed. Yes, it was rewarded."

"The William Marshal Academy is not weird," Edwin said with feigned severity.

"Your students put on Shakespeare plays for the fun of it. There are approximately zero computers in the entire school. The whole place looks more like an abbey than a school. Oh, and a crazy woman is wandering around at night. And you say Marshal isn't weird? You and I need to have a long talk about the definitions of *interesting* and *weird*. We are living in opposite lands."

"First of all, the Bride isn't a crazy woman."

"I know."

"You do?"

"She's one of the boy's girlfriends, isn't she?"

"I can't comment."

"I'll take that as a yes," Gwen said.

"Gwendolyn." His voice was stern.

"What?" she asked with a wicked grin.

And just like that, they were making love for a third time that night. Afterward, he pulled her close to his chest again and she fell asleep, wrapped in his arms.

———

It felt like only a few minutes had passed when light through the curtains woke her the next morning. Edwin was still asleep. She extricated herself carefully from his arms and wrapped herself in the Oxford shirt she'd practically ripped off of him last night. She pulled back a corner of the curtains and peered through the window. An autumnal fog covered the grounds of the school. The grass, the trees, even the other buildings were shrouded in gauze. The world had turned white.

Soon the boys would wake and start to stir. She needed to hurry back to her cottage now before anyone saw her leaving the headmaster's quarters. They wouldn't be able to keep their love affair a secret for long, but she wasn't overly worried. The boys adored their headmaster and had even conspired to find him a girlfriend.

No, not a girlfriend. A wife.

A wife? What the hell was she getting herself into?

Gwen dressed quickly and left a note for Edwin on the bedside table.

Headmaster Yorke—

You are a heavy sleeper. Yet another of your many faults. If you'd been awake, you could have had me again before I slipped out of your life forever. By "forever" I mean until I see you again later today. I adore you.

Sincerely, Miss Ashby

PS—Tea later? And by tea, I mean...not tea.

She kissed him softly on the lips. It broke her heart to know his first lover had treated him like a mere body and hadn't even kissed him on the mouth during their trysts. And then he'd been pressured by his family into marrying a woman who never could have loved him. She pitied his ex-wife, but it still seemed so unfair to Edwin.

Gwen was determined to make up for all the lost time, all the rejection, all the hurt. She would kiss him and touch him and pleasure him every chance she could. And although she feared it would be the most foolish of ideas, she would love him if he wanted her to love him.

She made sure she looked as put together as possible on the off-chance someone was out this early. But she saw no one as she left the main building by the back door and headed to her cottage. She was nearly there when she saw a flash of white out of the corner of her eye.

She stopped and spun around. Nothing to see. The campus was quiet, serene in the early-morning fog. But surely she hadn't imagined that rustle of white fabric in her peripheral vision...

There. Movement, on the back porch of the Pembroke dormitory.

The Bride.

The woman was less than fifty feet from her, facing away from Gwen and looking toward the sky. Slender and tall, she had the bearing of a young woman.

Gwen opened her mouth to call out to the girl. Before she could speak a word, someone joined the Bride on the back porch. A boy. From the back, she couldn't tell who it was because of his baseball cap. But she could see him reach for the Bride's hand.

She saw no one as she left the main building by the back door and headed to her cottage. She was nearly there when she saw a flash of white out of the corner of her eye.

That did it. Now Gwen was certain. The Bride was no bride at all. Just a girl in a dress sneaking on and off campus to see a boyfriend. Gwen wasn't sure why she wore the wedding dress as a disguise. Maybe if she kept up the ghostly ruse, the other boys would keep their distance? Teenagers were weird. No doubt about that.

Less worried now, Gwen left the young lovers alone. She'd keep digging around for more information on the girl. It might not hurt to find out which boy she was sneaking on campus to see. The last thing Gwen wanted was a Marshal student getting a townie pregnant. As if this school hadn't been through enough.

Young love. Almost as powerful as not-so-young love.

Love? Was she already using that word?

How long had she been here? Only a week? She knew couples who had fallen in love fast. Her parents had. Her father told her he knew he'd marry her mom on their very first date.

Still, it was strange how quickly she'd come to love this place and feel at home here. She hadn't once gone to her car to inspect the damage from the accident. What was the point? She'd do it later. Right now, she wanted to curl up in bed, catch up on the sleep she'd missed last night, and dream of Edwin.

Cars could wait.

Ghosts could wait.

The outside world could wait.

Sleep couldn't.

And love. Love couldn't wait either.

So she fell in love when she fell into bed and woke up a few hours later still in both.

CHAPTER ELEVEN

The next week passed in a haze of teaching and reading and Edwin and happiness. Gwen worked with the boys in small groups during her free period in the hopes of getting them to open up to her. She was on the lookout for any hint of which one of the boys was sneaking a girl onto campus. They all seemed to have baseball caps, so that one clue wasn't a damn bit of help. Their necks betrayed no hickeys or love bites. Their smiles betrayed no secrets. She could only hope whichever student had the girlfriend was being careful.

Careful? Good question. Did they teach sex ed at this school? Seemed like an entirely reasonable thing to do. She should ask the headmaster about it. And she should insist that he teach the class himself and that she be allowed to sit in and watch while Edwin lectured about penises and vaginas to thirty teenage boys.

Once the school day ended, Gwen walked up to the fourth floor of Hawkwood and found Edwin in his office.

She shut the door behind her and Edwin looked up.

"You're smiling," he said. "Stop it."

"I can't. It just happens when I'm in the same room with you."

He gave her a stern look, which failed to snuff out her smile. "I hope you're here to discuss work."

"I am."

"Good."

"And sex."

"Not good."

"Do we teach sex ed at Marshal?"

"Sex ed?" he asked. "You mean health class?"

"I guess you could call it that if you needed a euphemism," she said. "But specifically sexual education. There's at least one boy on campus with a girlfriend."

"Not this again."

"This again," she said, coming around his desk. It was a big desk, a grand desk, an impressive, manly desk. Thus she felt perfectly justified in sitting on it and crossing her legs right in front of Edwin's face.

"We don't need to teach sex to the boys," he said.

"I'm not saying we teach them the best way to do doggy style. But they should know about birth control and STIs."

"STIs?"

"You know—gonorrhea, syphilis, HIV…"

"Venereal diseases."

"Those," she said, amused by his tenacious clinging to

old-fashioned terminology. He even called the bathroom "the water closet" once. Adorable.

"It's hardly anything we need to be concerned about."

"Edwin, it's very sweet that you think the boys are all virgins who will be angels until the day they get married, but this is the real world. Teenagers have sex almost as often as adults do. And let's see...we've had sex..." She paused. "Three times on Friday, three times on Saturday, twice on Sunday. Day of rest, I understand. And then Monday night, Tuesday night, Wednesday—"

He raised his hand. "No need to tally it up," he said, suppressing a smile. "I was there, too."

"You were, weren't you? If the two of us are having this much sex, how much do you think a bunch of teenage boys awash in hormones are?"

"I'm not saying they're all monks, Gwendolyn. But there's no reason to worry about them."

"I'm not worried. I just think they need to know more than Latin and geometry. There is more to life than school," she said, uncrossing her legs and putting a foot on either side of his thighs. "Wouldn't you agree?"

"Gwendolyn." Edwin gave her a cold, hard stare.

"Edwin," she replied, smiling seductively.

"This is highly inappropriate."

"I locked the door when I came in."

He continued to stare at her. And then, just like that, he stood up, took off his glasses, grabbed her by the hips and pulled her to the very edge of the desk.

"Edwin!" she gasped in shock, but he silenced her with a kiss. Forget the boys. The man should teach sex ed to the entire world. He'd amazed her with his skills as a lover. He never let her go to bed still wanting more, and as soon as she woke up, she wanted him again.

Again. Always. And now.

Especially now.

"Are you absolutely entirely certain you locked the door?" Edwin whispered in her ear. She didn't know what it was—the accent most likely—that made his whispers as erotic as his touch.

"I promise I did."

"Good."

And with that *good,* he unbuttoned her blouse. But he didn't stop with unbuttoning it. He pulled it completely off. He then proceeded to strip her naked, completely naked but for the pale pink kitten heels on her feet. Edwin's large, strong hands roved all over her body. As he kissed her again on the mouth, he took her breasts into his hands. He pinched and rolled her nipples between his fingers until she panted against his lips.

He laughed softly and shushed her at the same time. Unless they were in his bedroom, they had to make every effort to be as quiet as possible. But it wasn't easy to stay silent when Edwin massaged her breasts like that, when his hips ground against hers, when his mouth caressed her neck in that spot that made her tense and tingle.

Edwin cupped her between her thighs and pushed a finger inside her. She pushed against his hand, craving more. He pushed a second finger in and her vagina tightened around him.

"God, Gwen," he said against her skin. She loved these little moments when he was so turned on he called her

Gwen instead of Gwendolyn. It was Edwin's version of losing control.

She reached between their bodies and unzipped Edwin's pants. With both hands, she stroked him to his full hardness. He closed his eyes and tilted his head back while she touched him. It was a beautiful thing to see him lost in his pleasure, the pleasure she gave to him.

Gwen let him go long enough to grasp the fabric of his jacket and push it off his shoulders. She yanked his tie off and unbuttoned his shirt halfway down. She didn't care about getting him naked right now as long as she could kiss and touch his chest and shoulders. She needed his skin against her skin as much as she needed him inside her. He must have felt the same, because he gripped her hard by the hips again, and, with both hands, pried her thighs wide open.

He lowered his head and pressed his tongue inside her. The sensation was exquisite, but the act unnecessary. She was already wet and ready for him.

Edwin rose and wrapped an arm around her waist, cushioning her as she rolled onto her back. He lifted her legs over his shoulders and with a thrust entered her. She raised her hips to take all of him into her. Briefly, she wondered what important paperwork they were on top of and possibly getting wet. But then he pulled out and thrust in again, hard and deep, and she decided she didn't care if they were fucking on top of the original draft of the Magna Carta itself as long as he kept...doing...*that*.

She half-closed her eyes and let herself bask in the heat of her own body and the hardness of his inside her.

But her erotic reverie dissipated when she heard Edwin saying her name.

"Gwendolyn?"

She opened her eyes and looked up at him. "Edwin?"

"You'll stay, won't you? No matter what happens? You'll stay here with me?"

His voice was quiet, serious. He seemed to be saying more than his words revealed. She rolled up and put her arms around his neck, pulling him close. He thrust into her again as she wrapped her legs around his back, clinging to him out of pure desire.

"I shouldn't ask you to stay," he said, stroking her hair, kissing her neck. "You don't even know what you're giving up. But please…"

"I'll stay," she said, making the promise so easily she couldn't imagine why he'd called it a sacrifice. For Edwin she would stay. For the boys. For the love of teaching and the love of learning and the love of the life she'd been granted here like a wish she didn't remember making.

It was a wish. It was a dream. It was everything she'd wanted and hadn't ever dared to ask for. And here it was, in her hands. And she would never let it go.

Locked in each other's arms, they moved together and against each other and with each other, until finally she shuddered in his arms and he came inside her body. And yet still they held each other, moved by the pledge she'd made him, knowing what it meant without even needing to say it.

Edwin was in love with her, too.

And she would never leave him.

Never.

CHAPTER TWELVE

Gwen spent a good hour on Edwin's lap in his office after they'd finished making love on his desk. They were fully dressed, unfortunately. They didn't want to push their luck. And with that thought in mind, Gwen finally summoned the courage to say what had to be said.

"We should tell the boys," she said.

"Tell them what?"

"That we are a *we*."

Edwin looked at her, aghast. "We should?"

"We are a *we*, aren't we? Or are we not a *we*?"

She tensed waiting for his reply.

"We are," he said. "We certainly are. We are also an *us*."

"Good. Then we should tell the boys before they figure it out on their own. Better to hear it from we—I mean, from us. Otherwise, the rumors will start flying."

"They are nosy gossips. Typical Americans."

"Especially Laird."

"He's likely already planning our wedding."

"He loves you like a father," Gwen said. "He wants to see you happy."

"I am happy," Edwin said. "You on my lap in my office... I have died and gone to Heaven. Or a reasonable facsimile."

"I didn't know they had sex this good in Heaven. I'll need to rethink my theology."

"Wouldn't be Heaven otherwise."

She gave him a heavenly kiss goodbye and left him to his work. They'd only slightly soiled Edwin's desk blotter. No report cards or term papers had been harmed.

Gwen returned to her cottage, graded papers, and had dinner in the dining hall with Mr. Price and Mr. Reynolds. After dinner, she went for a walk around campus. She spent an hour trying to figure out a way to tell the students—and the other staff—she and the headmaster were a couple. Had it been a larger school, it wouldn't have mattered. But everyone knew everyone here. By her count, there were thirty-four people at the school, adults and children. No keeping secrets in a school so small. She'd much rather be open and honest about their relationship than keep sneaking around, waiting for someone to catch them kissing or holding hands...or worse.

Laird.

That was it. Of course Laird. He couldn't keep a secret to save his life. That gossipy twerp was just who she needed. Next time he asked about her and the headmaster—probably tomorrow—she'd tell him the truth. A heavily edited and family-friendly version of the truth, of course. And by dinner, everyone on campus would know. Probably everyone within a fifty-mile radius.

Gwen walked back to her cottage and took a long bath. When she checked the clock, she saw it was hardly past nine. If she was good and asked very nicely, maybe she could talk Edwin into a repeat of today's performance, but in his bed instead of on his hard office desk.

She peeked out her front door. First, she looked left. Then she looked right. Then she looked toward the dormitories. No one seemed to be out and about. She was safe to jog over to Hawkwood and hunt the headmaster down. After how good he'd made her feel today, she thought she should return the favor. It was the only ladylike thing to do.

The image of giving Edwin another ladylike blow job put a grin on Gwen's face and preoccupied her so thoroughly that she almost didn't notice the lady in white standing motionless near the wall. But when Gwen did see her, she decided that now—right now—she'd get to the bottom of the mystery. Gwen didn't care that the Bride was dating one of the boys in secret. What she worried about was this girl sneaking on and off campus at all hours of the night. It wasn't safe. Not out here in the middle of nowhere when there were venomous snakes and black bears and who-knew-what-else in the hills.

"Miss?" Gwen called out as she neared her. "Miss, can I talk to you?"

She expected the Bride might run. What she didn't expect was how fast the Bride could run. Before Gwen could even react, the girl was off like a shot. Was she wearing sneakers under her skirt? Gwen took off after her, although she had no hope of closing the widening gap. The Bride was sprinting like a track star, bounding easily over every rock and stone in her path. Gwen could only watch as the girl disappeared around the corner of Newbury, knowing that when she, too, rounded the corner, the Bride would be long gone in the darkness.

And that's exactly what happened. Gwen was left standing in the school courtyard in the moonlight, catching her breath. Where on earth had the girl gone? She couldn't have just disappeared into thin air. Had she scaled the school wall in that dress, or was she simply lying in wait until Gwen gave up her pursuit?

With her heart pounding from the chase, Gwen walked back to Pembroke where she'd first seen the Bride. There were a few footprints in the soft soil, but nothing else.

Actually...there *was* something else, on the porch. A scrap of white fabric caught on a nail. Gwen pulled it free and studied it.

White. Lacy. Embroidered. It wasn't fabric from the dress, as she'd first assumed. It was a handkerchief. She sensed no magic in it, no ghostly presence. It didn't even smell of a woman's perfume.

Gwen turned it over and noticed a tiny set of initials sewn into one corner. She recognized the initials in an instant and knew something was very wrong at the William Marshal Academy.

She'd hoped the girl was simply a girlfriend.

Now Gwen knew better.

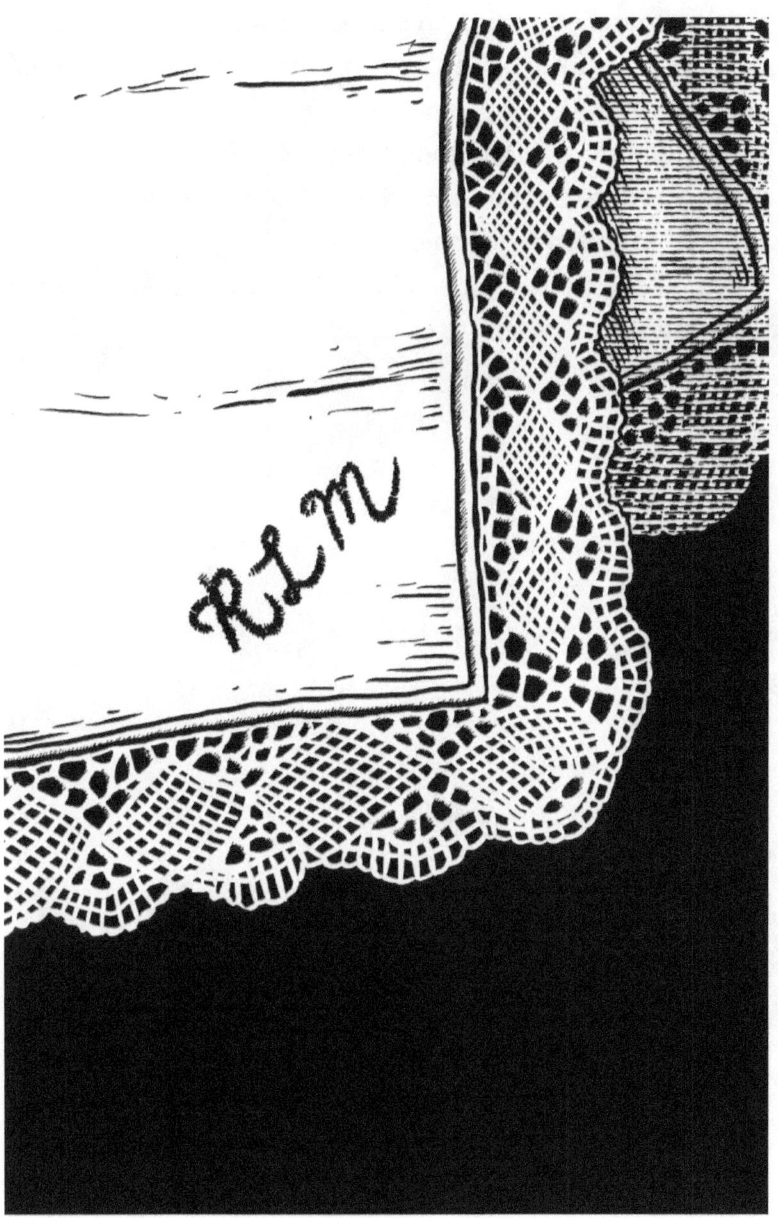

She recognized the initials in an instant and knew something was very wrong at the William Marshal Academy.

She marched to Edwin's quarters and knocked on his door. When a knock didn't get his attention, she pounded on it.

Edwin threw the door open. He wore silk pajama pants, his dressing gown, and a look of consternation.

"Gwendolyn, what on earth—"

"Call the police," she said. "That teacher, Miss Muir? She's sneaking back onto campus."

CHAPTER THIRTEEN

Gwen sat across from Edwin at the kitchen table. He'd ordered her to calm down and drink her tea.

"You haven't called the police yet," she said.

The look of consternation hadn't left his face. "You haven't touched your tea," he said.

"I'll drink it if you promise to call the police after I finish it."

"I'm not going to call the police, Gwendolyn. There is no reason to involve any outsiders in this matter."

"I saw her at the boys' dorms, Edwin. I can't believe you would be so cavalier about the safety of the students."

"I would die for these boys and you know that. But I know more about this situation than you do. It's not something I can discuss."

"You can't discuss the fact that a crazy ex-teacher is roaming around the school in a bridal gown?"

"Miss Muir is not roaming around the school."

"Then why did I find a handkerchief with her initials on it? It was on the porch of the dorm. *R.L.M.* Rosemary Leigh Muir. I saw her name and her initials in the Bible she left behind in the cottage. She is nuts, and she is dangerous, and she is clearly still on campus."

"She is not mad, and she is not on campus. She left and is not coming back. I swear that to you on my honor."

She ignored both his swearing and his honor. "What did Miss Muir look like? Can you tell me that?" Gwen demanded.

Edwin shrugged. "She was a woman. She had a woman's features."

Gwen rolled her eyes. "Hair? Did she have any hair?"

"Yes."

"What color was it? Black? White? Blond? Red?"

"Black and long, if I remember correctly. Does that put your mind at ease?"

Not really, Gwen thought. She hadn't actually seen the Bride's hair under the veil. Even if she had, hair could be cut, dyed.

"Miss Muir is gone," Edwin continued. "I don't know how many more times I can tell you that. She left to get married."

Gwen threw her hands up. "Who quits working just to get married? My mom didn't even do that in the seventies."

"Miss Muir did."

"What's her married name?" Gwen asked, hoping to wring some information out of Edwin. "Is there a phone book around here? I want to call her."

"I'm sorry, I have no information on her whereabouts at this time."

"So she could be here, for all you know."

"She could not," Edwin said.

Gwen's hands balled up in angry fists. "I can't believe you're being like this. This isn't a secret you're allowed to keep from me. It involves the safety of the students. *My* students."

"I am fully aware of that. If I thought the presence of this person on campus was in any way something I should concern myself with, then I would concern myself with it. It is not, however. You'll simply have to trust me. As I've said, I am not at liberty to discuss it."

That was not the answer she wanted or needed. She put her tea back on her saucer and stood up. "I want to trust you, Edwin, but I can't. Not with this."

"I'm very sorry to hear that," he said, and her heart broke at the sorrow in his voice, the regret.

"If you change your mind and decide you can tell me what's going on, you know where to find me," she said. "Until you decide to tell me, I would appreciate it if you didn't come to my cottage. And I won't be coming here either."

"I understand," he said, his voice now stony and stoic when just today it had been so heated and heartfelt.

Without another word, she turned and left him alone at the kitchen table.

———

INSTEAD OF HEADING STRAIGHT BACK to her cottage, she walked the school grounds hoping to find more evidence. She had the handkerchief. Surely there were clues out here to be found, even at this hour. What else was she going to do, sleep? That wasn't happening, not with her mind pre-occupied with the Bride's identity.

Around and around campus she walked until her feet were tired. Anger kept her on the move. Why didn't Edwin trust her with the truth, whatever it was? She thought he'd trusted her. He'd told her about his first lover, his wife. The truth about his divorce. Those were all aspects of his past she'd wanted to know, but nothing she'd *needed* to know. This she needed to know. And yet no amount of begging and pleading had gotten the truth out of him.

What was he hiding? And why was he hiding it?

But those questions were the least of her concerns. What mattered more than anything was keeping the boys on campus safe from harm. And Edwin didn't seem at all worried about the madwoman roaming campus. Fine, she'd protect the students herself if she had to.

She returned to her cottage and sat at her kitchen table. She had nothing but questions. What she needed were answers. If Miss Muir were still living on campus, Gwen knew she would need things—food, water, a place to shower, a place to sleep. Well, Edwin had told her half the student body had been pulled out by their parents so that meant there were empty rooms in the dorms. All right, that was a possibility. But surely the boys would have noticed by now?

What if she hadn't moved into an empty dorm room,

then. What if she'd never actually left the cottage in the first place? A chill of apprehension passed through Gwen's body. Was she sharing her home with an intruder? She'd heard horror stories in the news about people secretly living in attics, in basements...

The cottage sat empty for nine hours every weekday. Breakfast was at eight. Classes started at nine. Lunch at one. Gwen had her last afternoon class at three. She didn't return to the cottage until five at the earliest. Was Miss Muir—or whoever she was—sneaking into Gwen's cottage to sleep or eat or bathe during the week?

With a rush of adrenaline, Gwen tore through every room, examining every closet, every nook and cranny. She saw no signs that anyone was living here but her. Cold comfort that, but it was something.

Maybe Miss Muir wasn't living on campus. Maybe just visiting campus frequently. Why would an old teacher sneak onto campus?

The worst possibility seemed the most likely—that she'd seduced one of the boys and was engaging in a relationship with him. Vile, but it wouldn't have been the first time in history. Yet Gwen knew if that were the case, Edwin would've called in the authorities.

Edwin had been adamant the Bride wasn't Miss Muir. Was the woman in the white dress homeless? Gwen could easily see Edwin or the boys taking pity on someone with nowhere else to go. That was hardly something Edwin would keep a secret from her, though. And, despite Edwin's protestations, Gwen couldn't shake the terrible feeling that Miss Muir was involved in some way. Gut instinct? Something in the air? Just a bad, bad feeling?

Even if she wasn't the Bride, the ex-teacher had some role in whatever was happening at Marshal Academy.

Gwen took Miss Muir's Bible out from the desk drawer again. People used to store photographs and letters in the pages of Bibles. It was worth checking.

Carefully, she turned the onionskin pages. Back at Savannah State, Gwen had taught a seminar on the poetry of the Bible—the Psalms, the Song of Solomon. The "Fun Books," as her students called them. Miss Muir didn't seem interested in "the fun books," but the lists of rules in the Old Testament had certainly captured the woman's attention. The word *abomination* was circled over and over again. Every occurrence, from the looks of it.

Eating pork and shellfish was an abomination.

Trimming one's beard was an abomination.

Cross-dressing was an abomination.

A man lying with a man was an abomination.

That last verse had been underlined, too—not once but twice. And starred.

Fine, then. If Miss Muir was like that, then tonight Gwen would eat oysters for dinner while wearing pants and reading gay erotica.

The fact still remained that she knew so little about Miss Muir. Edwin had told her almost nothing. Maybe the boys would be more talkative.

———

GWEN WENT into class on Monday morning prepared to begin *A Midsummer Night's Dream*. What she wasn't fully prepared for were the ten apples on her desk and a

Welcome to Marshal banner strung across her chalkboard.

Her eyes filled with tears as she smiled at the class.

"No, don't do that," Laird said. "No crying. We'll take the apples back if you start crying."

"I won't cry," she said, crying.

"There was a note hanging in the dorms that said you were the new official teacher of literature at Marshal. We might have been happy to see that," Christopher said.

"No more *Ivanhoe!*" Jefferson yelled, and the class applauded and hooted.

"This is very sweet of you all," she said. "You didn't have to spend your weekend making me a welcome sign."

"We're stuck at an all-boys school," Christopher sighed. "We had to find something to do on Saturday. It was either make a sign or burn the dorms down."

"Not funny," Laird said, elbowing him.

"I'm glad you spent it making me a sign instead of engaging in criminal behavior," Gwen said.

"Hope you found something fun to do over the weekend," Laird said, his voice a little too innocent for her liking.

She narrowed her eyes at him. "I prepared lectures and notes all weekend. I didn't burn anything down."

"So you didn't have any fun, Miss Ashby? None at all?" Laird asked.

"None," she promised. "Teachers don't have any fun. Ever."

Laird nodded. "Of course. Right. No fun at all."

"None. Now speaking of no fun, let's get to work."

She turned around and started to write this week's

lesson plan on the board. As soon as her back was turned, she heard one of the boys put on a perfect female falsetto and gasp, "Edwin!"

Her piece of chalk froze on the board as the entire class burst into giggles.

Gwen blushed so scarlet that she felt the heat all the way to her bones. But that was okay. She took a deep breath and reminded herself these were teenage boys. It was only a matter of time before her little angels showed their devilish side.

"Actually, before we start our new book, let's do something fun," she said. "Take out some paper, boys. We're having a test."

She turned and glared at Laird, who had already proven he could do a good falsetto during the play.

"We're taking our welcome sign back," Christopher said, sliding down in his seat with a frown.

At the end of class, Gwen got even more revenge on the boys.

"Laird, Christopher, stay behind a moment," she said.

The boys froze in obvious terror. The class gave them looks of sympathy on their way out.

As soon as they were alone in the room, Laird started. "I'm sorry, Miss Ashby. I didn't mean...it wasn't me," he lied. "I just—"

"You're not in trouble," she said. "Neither are you, Laird. I'm guessing certain things were overheard?"

"Um..." Christopher said. "Yes. But we're really happy for you. And Headmaster Yorke. He's a catch. Good job."

"I'm not going to talk about Headmaster Yorke with you two."

"No offense, Miss Ashby, but you don't have to," Laird said. Then he lowered his voice. "We already know."

She ran her fingers over her lips to zip them.

"Fine," Laird said and zipped his lips.

"The reason I asked you two to stay, other than the fact that you're both scared of me—"

"Only a little," Christopher said.

"I wanted to ask you something. What do you know about Miss Muir?"

Christopher and Laird went dead silent and gave each other looks. Strange looks that she couldn't read.

"What?" Gwen asked. "Tell me."

Christopher shrugged. "Nothing to tell. She was here for a couple of years. She taught our lit classes. She was here one day and gone the next."

Gwen turned to Laird. "And do you know anything about what happened to her?"

"The headmaster said she left to get married."

"Are you sure?" Gwen asked. She had the feeling the boys were hiding something from her. "Is there anything else you can tell me about her?"

"She read the Bible a lot," Christopher said. "But her classes were okay."

"Pretty okay," Laird said. "Yours are better."

"You said she didn't like you much," Gwen reminded them.

"We talk a lot," Christopher said. "Maybe that was it. I mean, what else would it be? We're adorable."

He and Laird put their hands under their chins and batted their eyelashes at her.

She sighed. "Thank you, I think. I'll see you later. And,

guys, please try to contain your enthusiasm for my private life."

Laird grinned unrepentantly at her. "We'll try, but as you know, we don't have private lives of our own. We have to get our kicks somewhere."

"Kick elsewhere," she warned.

"Yes, Miss Ashby," Christopher said, and he and Laird left.

She looked out at the empty classroom. Miss Muir had sat in this same chair behind this same desk and stared at the same rows of tables and chairs. Did the woman like teaching here? Did she love the students? Was she nice to them? Fair? Cruel? Indifferent?

Gwen opened the desk drawer and found it as empty as she'd found it last week. No pens. No paper. No nothing, not even clear in the back. Miss Muir hadn't just taken her personal stuff, she'd taken every last supply. Unless she'd kept her things somewhere else...

At that, Gwen remembered something Edwin had shown her on her very first day here at Marshal. Something she'd completely forgotten.

"I have an office."

CHAPTER FOURTEEN

Gwen headed upstairs to Miss Muir's old office but didn't go inside, not at first. She didn't know why she felt nervous opening the door. Did she think she'd find the Bride in there, sitting behind the desk? *Pull it together,* she told herself, then took a deep breath and opened the door.

Nothing greeted her but sunlight through the window and dust motes dancing in the air.

And the scent of smoke.

Gwen coughed, covered her nose and mouth with her hand. Where was the smell coming from? She threw open the window and scanned the grounds. No flames, no ash. No smoke clouding the sky. No evidence of fire, not as far as the eye could see.

Where there's smoke there's fire, they say, but Gwen couldn't find either. Only that smoky scent, which dissipated as she aired the office out.

Bizarre. Where on earth had the smell come from? Surely she hadn't imagined it. This was the second time she'd smelled smoke on campus and hadn't been able to find its source.

Gwen surveyed the office. In the center sat a small writing desk. A lady's desk, ornate and delicate. A stark contrast to Edwin's massive oak desk that one woman could lay on very comfortably. Gwen examined the papers on the desk. Some had writing on them but they seemed to be nothing but little class notes.

Test on Thursday.

Grades due May 1st.

Order the new Robert Frost.

Gwen furrowed her brow. A new Frost biography or new compilation? Robert Frost hadn't released any new poems in half a century. He'd been dead since 1963.

In a desk drawer, she found Miss Muir's grading book. There they were—all thirty current students. Russell Adams. Eliot Bryant. Joshua Charles. Laird Donnelly. Marcus Farrell, Christopher Hayes. And on and on. She smiled at their names. She could put a face to each name now, and a personality to each face. Christopher and Laird were golden-hearted troublemakers—best friends for life. Samuel, the only Black student at the school and easily the most intelligent student. He'd started talking more in her class, and she was amazed by his insight into human psychology. Eliot was quiet and bookish but with a dry wit. Joshua cared far more for math than English but still did his best for her. Good boys, all of them. Well trained by the headmaster.

Under the grade book, Gwen found a printed list of

the students' addresses. Only twenty-nine names. She put the handwritten grade book next to the name and address list and ticked off the names side by side. It didn't take long to find the missing boy.

Laird Alexander Donnelly. How odd. He appeared on the class grade book but not on the school roster? That made no sense. Things just weren't adding up around here.

Gwen dug further, but could find nothing else suspicious or strange in the drawers. What stood out, however, was how much stuff Miss Muir had left behind. She had pens in her desk that would have sold for a fortune in an antique pen store. Old Montblanc pens still in excellent working condition. Even if they were, in fact, school property, who didn't pocket a few office supplies when leaving their job?

The office bookshelves were stuffed with hardbound early editions of dozens of classics. An embarrassment of riches. Gwen ran her hands over the covers of the books. *Pride and Prejudice. Emma.* And Edwin's favorite, *Ivanhoe.* If they were Miss Muir's—being unmarked, they weren't library copies—she had simply left them behind when she'd quit.

She opened *Ivanhoe*, curious about why it held such a place in Edwin's heart. The boys had been forced to read this book more than once after he had taken over Miss Muir's class. She knew little about the book except the main character was a twelfth-century knight, and it was considered a Romance in the classic sense of the word—a story with a hero who goes on a noble quest and upholds the ideas of chivalry. She flipped through the pages.

*She sat at the desk and read through the letter once,
then twice, then a third time simply to convince herself
to believe what her eyes told her.*

Gwen found an interesting passage that she read aloud. *"For he that does good, having the unlimited power to do evil, deserves praise not only for the good which he performs, but for the evil which he forbears."*

Yeah. That sounded like annoyingly noble Edwin. No wonder he loved it.

A page fell out of the book as Gwen continued to leaf through it. Well, that just killed the resale value of the book. She picked the page off the floor and saw it wasn't a page from the book but the draft of a letter.

A letter to Edwin.

She sat down at the desk. She read through the letter once, then twice, then a third time simply to convince herself to believe what her eyes told her. And yet, she still couldn't believe it. Many words and lines were blotted out as if Miss Muir had been struggling with her words.

Headmaster Yorke,

By the time you read this note, I will be gone. I can no longer abide the sin and licentiousness you have allowed to flourish on your watch. Evil is here, and the souls of the boys are at stake. Sin is a disease and I cannot stay here lest I be infected. God will smite this school in His wrath and vengeance with fire and death if you do not tear out the evil that has taken root here. This is not merely a matter of conscience. This is a grave and

present danger. By allowing this evil to flourish, you have put the entire school at risk. I
will contact the parents since you refuse to do
your duty. May God have mercy on your soul.

In the name of the Lord,
Rosemary Muir

Gwen's hand shook as she read the note. What sin was she talking about? What evil had come to this school that Miss Muir was so certain would destroy the boys in a fiery conflagration? She sounded crazy with all this talk of God's wrath and sin that spread like a disease. And yet something had set her off. What had she seen or heard that had scared her so profoundly that she thought she had to run away from the school and contact the parents?

Had Miss Muir written out a clean copy, or was this the only draft, unsent and unseen by Edwin?

———

Gwen found Edwin sitting at his desk in his office, his door open. He had a pen in hand and a ledger in front of him.

"I have to talk to you," she said.

He glanced up from his work. She saw a fleeting expression of pleasure in his eyes at the unexpected sight of her.

"Close the door, please."

"I don't know if that's a good idea," she whispered. "The boys overheard us."

"Overheard us?" he asked, sitting back in his chair.

"Friday. I mean, they heard me saying your name," she said as she seated herself in the chair in front of his desk. A blush suffused her cheeks. "They made that very clear in class."

Edwin's eyes widened. "I certainly hope you disciplined them. That is unacceptable behavior for young gentlemen."

"I gave them a pop quiz. A vicious one."

"Good. You aren't here to talk about...us?"

"No," she said and noted the disappointment lurking at the corners of his mouth. He must have been missing her as much as she was missing him. "I was in my office just now. Miss Muir's office. I found this in a copy of *Ivanhoe.* Can you tell me what this is about?"

She unfolded the note and passed it to him.

"First, you have to tell me why you were reading *Ivanhoe,*" he said.

"I was scanning it for sex scenes. Now read the letter."

He glanced it over. "Appears to be a draft of a letter."

"Did you receive the final draft?" she asked.

"I did."

"And?"

"I burned it."

"Why?"

"Because it was full of rambling nonsense that I had no time for. She left the school. She's gone. We moved on," Edwin said, folding the paper with a dismissive crease.

"What on earth was she talking about in this letter? Sin? Evil? Wrath of God?"

"Miss Muir was a fanatically religious woman. She saw sin everywhere," Edwin said, sounding disgusted.

"She saw sin here at this school, and she said you knew about it."

"I don't see sin at this school, Miss Ashby. I see young men who are doing their very best. They require discipline and compassion. And learning. That is all."

"I see the same thing," she said. "I've never seen a group of students so devoted to each other."

"They would die for each other," Edwin said. "And if any of them were in trouble or in danger, the administration would be the first to know."

"Are you sure about that? Are you sure they would trust us?"

"They trust me, Miss Ashby. And when they have troubles and fears they bring them to me. You're new. You're a woman. It will take time before they can trust you with their private concerns. I'm well aware of what's going on with the boys on this campus, which is why I tell you there is no cause for you to worry and no reason to give Miss Muir another thought."

"I want to believe that," Gwen said, "but I can't." She stood and turned for the door, but stopped when he called her name.

"Gwendolyn."

She slowly turned around.

"Close the door," he said. "Please."

She heard the somber tone in his voice and did as he asked.

"What?" she said as soon as the door was closed.

"Gwendolyn…" Edwin repeated, and paused to collect himself. "These past few days together…they've meant something to me. I told you things I've never told anyone. And we shared the deepest, most private, most intimate acts two people could share."

She swallowed hard. "I know."

"Did our nights mean anything to you? What we said to each other? What we did to each other?"

Gwen sighed as she wrapped her arms over her stomach. "Yes, it meant more than I can tell you."

She walked back to his desk and sat again in the chair. She couldn't meet his eyes.

"I've never been a romantic soul," she continued. "The gap between what I read in novels and what happens in the real world… My parents are dead, just like Pip's in *Great Expectations*. Where's my mysterious wealthy benefactor? I had to pay my own way through school. We're out here in the woods far from the city. Where are Oberon and Titania and all their magic spells? The real world and the world of fiction are far apart. And that's how it should be. All fiction is aspirational. At least…I thought that until I met you. You read books about love at first sight, but I never believed it was real."

Gwen looked at Edwin and smiled.

"Then you…" Gwen continued. "I woke up in your bed and you gave me a job and a place to live and I'm lost. I'm lost in what I feel for you. And then we made love and I was even more lost. Edwin, I'm so lost a map and a compass and a whole pack of bloodhounds couldn't find me again."

Edwin took off his glasses and sat them on this desk. He clasped his hands and met her eyes.

"I am lost, too, Gwendolyn. I have never...had what you and I have had even for this short time. And you arrive here, the last place you should be, and here I am. Lost in the one place that ever felt like home to me. I want you back in my bed. Now. Tonight. Forever. But you have to trust me. I trusted you."

"Edwin..." Gwen whispered and closed her eyes. A thousand images flashed across her mind's eye. Edwin kissing her, touching her, pushing inside her. The way his eyes glowed with desire when he pulled her into his bedroom. She was safe in his arms. He belonged inside her. She'd never felt anything so right.

"Please trust me, Gwendolyn. Please trust that I know what I'm doing. Please believe in me."

"I want to," she said. "But I could say the same to you. Trust me. Tell me what's going on. Tell me what you know."

"I can't. I simply can't. And I can't tell you why I can't. If I could tell you, I would, but to tell you would go against everything I believe and everything I stand for."

"Telling your lover the truth goes against everything you stand for? Then perhaps it's for the best we aren't lovers anymore."

"Perhaps it is," he said, his voice once more cold and stern. "But you must know, I wish it could be another way."

"It can be another way. This is your decision, Edwin."

He looked up at her with pleading eyes. But he said nothing, told her no secrets, revealed no answers.

She walked away.

———

THE REST OF THE DAY, Gwen put on a smile for the sake of her students. Her second and third-period classes went well. Not a single student teased her about the headmaster, and they all made it clear they were thrilled she would be staying at Marshal.

At the end of the day, she gathered her things and returned to Miss Muir's office, which was now hers. She proceeded to flip through every single page of every single book—a daunting task and one that was ultimately fruitless. Miss Muir had left notes in many of the books on the shelves, but they were nothing but class notes, lecture notes, or, in one case, a grocery list.

After hours of searching Miss Muir's office, Gwen returned to her cottage. Night had fallen. Before going inside she stood on the lawn and took in her new home, reminding herself that for all its problems, this job did come with a couple of very nice perks. She'd never dreamed she would ever live in a house so lovely. Teachers didn't make enough money to afford century-old Tudor-style cottages. The cottage itself was white but adorned with the standard dark decorative timbers on the outside. It looked like a home from a fairy tale, especially glowing as it did in the moonlight. Shakespeare might have lived in a house like this. Ivy climbed up one side almost to the chimney in knots and whorls so lush and thick it nearly covered a window on the north side.

A window? Gwen had never noticed ivy covering any

of her windows before. Not downstairs. Not upstairs. But there it was, a window high up on the side of the house. Gwen's heart raced with excitement. There was another room in her cottage somewhere. A secret room.

"Got you," she said aloud.

CHAPTER FIFTEEN

Gwen slipped off her shoes so her heels wouldn't make any sound on the hardwood. On bare feet, she headed up to the second floor. The window she'd seen obscured by ivy was high up. Very high. Higher than her bedroom window. That meant the house had either a third floor or an attic.

On the second floor, Gwen searched for a door she might have missed. She ran her fingers along the walls, looking for notches that might reveal a secret entrance or a break in the paneling. Nothing. And nothing in the master bedroom or the guest bedroom or the bathroom. But she refused to give up. There had to be a way up there. If she had to, she'd take a chainsaw to the ceiling.

The ceiling? What about the ceiling?

Gwen went through the entire second floor again, this time studying the ceiling for a hatch or pulldown door, the kind with a folded ladder like she'd seen in movies.

Still nothing.

She had to be missing something. She'd checked every room in the upstairs, even the closets. There had to be a way to this mysterious third floor or attic room. Then it dawned on her.

"I'm an idiot," she said, racing back down the stairs.

Of course there was a way to the third floor. But it wasn't through the second floor. If it was an old servants' quarters, it would have an entrance somewhere close to where food was prepared or served.

Back on the main floor, she headed straight for the kitchen. From there, she entered the pantry. And there, behind the boxes she'd been ignoring for a week, was a narrow door.

Everything in the pantry, including the door, was painted white, so she'd barely noticed it. She unlatched it, opened it, and saw a narrow staircase leading up into the darkness.

This was it.

But what was she about to walk into? Whatever it was, Gwen was not going up there in the dark unarmed.

She grabbed a kitchen knife. She looked everywhere for a flashlight with no luck. Instead, she took the oil lamp off the bedside table from upstairs, lit the wick with a match, and headed back for the pantry.

She stepped through the narrow door. Gwen held the lamp out in front of her, illuminating the staircase. Dust swirled around her, and she covered her mouth and nose to keep from sneezing.

She took a first tentative step. The wood creaked underfoot. Her heart was already racing, and the elderly stairs didn't help matters much.

She mounted each stair, testing it with her toes before putting her full weight on it.

Twenty-four steps later, she reached the door at the top.

Carefully she placed a hand on the knob. Dread consumed her. Light from the lamp danced across the door as her hand shook uncontrollably. The doorknob made no sound as she turned it.

In her head she counted *one...two...three...*

She threw the door open and screamed.

There she was. The Bride.

The woman stood still as death, back turned to Gwen in the darkened room. Just standing there in the shadows, all in white, unmoved by the armed intruder who had just let out a blood-curdling cry. Gwen couldn't see the woman's face underneath the veil, couldn't see any features other than the outline of the wedding dress.

"Ma'am?" Gwen whispered. "Miss?"

The Bride remained motionless, as if inviting her to make the first move.

Gwen had never been so scared in her life. She took a breath.

"Ma'am?" she said, louder this time.

No answer. Heart pounding, Gwen moved the lamp around to see the rest of the room. And that's all it was, a mostly empty room. A few bolts of cloth, a few small chairs, a rug. Summoning all her courage, she took the first step forward, alert for the woman to spin around at any moment.

Gwen took another step, then another. She thought her chest would burst from the frantic brutal beating of her heart. Her hands went clammy with terror as she crept around the Bride in a semi-circle, keeping a safe distance.

Finally, she was standing face-to-face with the Bride. Ten feet at most separated them. Gwen raised the lamp up high, bracing herself for whatever horrors the light revealed...

...and found that the woman had no face. She'd been prepared for many things, but not this.

There was no face because there was no woman. This wasn't the Bride. It was a mannequin—a seamstress's form, without arms. A wire held a bridal veil in place, a veil that veiled nothing when lifted.

The mannequin didn't even have a head.

"Oh my God..." Gwen breathed the words, nearly fainting from relief. There was a clatter as the knife slipped from her hand. She hadn't even realized she'd still had it.

The dress had a handmade quality to it, and needles and thread were strewn about a side table. Miss Muir had been using this room as a sewing room.

Edwin said she'd left the school to get married. What bride got married without her wedding dress, especially one she'd spent time hand-sewing? Either she hadn't left to get married...

...or Miss Muir hadn't left.

Gwen raced back down the stairs and out into the kitchen. She was covered with dust from her trek to the secret room, but she didn't stop to clean herself off.

The woman had no face. She'd been prepared for many things, but not this.

She'd go to Edwin right now and drag him by his ear to the room at the top of her house and show him Miss Muir's wedding dress. If he could look at that and still tell her to her face that Miss Muir had left to get married...

Gwen paused mid-thought. No. Maybe she wouldn't go to Edwin. Maybe she *shouldn't* go to Edwin. That letter had spoken of a danger, a grave and present danger. And Edwin had already made it clear he would do nothing about it. Fine. Let's see what the police had to say. If they couldn't reach Miss Muir, Gwen would tell the police her suspicions about where the woman was—still here, on campus, and up to no good. The only phone she'd seen was in the headmaster's quarters, which was out of the question. Her best bet was to drive into town, maybe stop at that diner where she'd gotten directions and use their phone.

Gwen headed to the small gravel lot outside the school grounds. Her car was the only one parked there. Where was Edwin's car? Mr. Price's? Had everyone abandoned her?

Something wasn't right. She couldn't see the other teachers leaving her alone on campus without giving her a heads up. In fact, she couldn't remember any of them talking about heading into town at any point since she'd arrived. Even stranger, this was the first time Gwen had even given the outside world a thought over the past week.

From the moment she'd arrived at Marshal, she hadn't wanted to leave. Not once. Not even to buy groceries for the cottage. She had all but forgotten about her friend in Chicago, who had to be wondering what had happened to her. What *was* happening to her? This school had sucked her in so thoroughly it was as if the outside world had ceased to exist once she'd started teaching here.

She had to get out. Now. She needed to get away from Edwin and the school for a few hours. Some distance would help her clear her head.

But when she finally reached her car, she gasped at the sight of it. She'd known it had been damaged when she hit the wall. Edwin had said she might not be able to drive it. But this was...

"Oh my God..." she breathed.

How had she survived this? The entire front end was smashed, glass shattered, and the steering wheel bent in an unnatural direction.

No...that couldn't be. She'd had a superficial head injury, and it had healed quickly. Someone had done something to her car. Taken it, driven it, and smashed it against a wall at a hundred miles an hour. Someone wanted to keep her trapped here. She wouldn't let them. She'd walk to town if she had to. She'd run.

She started to step out of the courtyard but then saw movement on the cobblestone.

A scream escaped her throat. She jerked her foot back.

A snake. A big one, black and coiled, lay on the road, guarding it like a one-headed Cerberus. Gwen peddled backward, fast.

When she'd put a safe distance between herself and the snake, Gwen turned to run.

And there she was. A flash of a white dress in the dark.

The Bride was on the move.

On pure instinct, and with a rush of terror and determination, Gwen raced for her, running as fast and as hard as she could. She would not let the Bride/Miss Muir elude her this time.

The Bride seemed to notice her but too late. Gwen grabbed a handful of the woman's hair as she descended the stone stairs from the turret.

Gwen stared down at the chunk of hair in her hand.

Then she saw the face of the Bride. The sheepish smiling wincing face...

"Laird?"

"Um...hi, Miss Ashby," he said. He gave her an awkward, embarrassed wave.

Her stomach nearly dropped out of the bottom of her feet at the shock and relief that it was Laird, only Laird, in a white dress...the same white dress that had been on the mannequin in her cottage only moments ago. The boy must have snuck in for it as soon as he'd seen her head out.

"What the hell are you doing out here, Laird? What is all this?" she demanded.

"Nothing. Just scaring the guys. Playing ghost. Just a trick. A prank," he said, his voice high-pitched and nervous.

"A prank? You scared the hell out of me. You've been scaring the hell out of me ever since I got here, sneaking around campus all in white like a ghost. What possessed you—"

"Laird?"

Gwen looked up at the sound of a familiar voice, a

voice with a slight stammer. It had come from inside the turret, where she could see a flickering light.

"Miss Ashby, look. I can explain," Laird said, grabbing her hand. Gwen pulled away from him and rushed up the stairs. "It's not what you think!"

At the top of the stairs was a small stone archway that led into the turret. And there inside the little room, no bigger than five feet across and five feet wide, sat not Miss Muir...but Christopher.

He was wearing boxer shorts and a white T-shirt. A small oil lamp burned at his side. She could see the seams of his T-shirt. It was inside out.

"Miss Ashby," he said, clearly shocked by her presence. "It's not—"

But it was. It was exactly what it looked like.

She heard a sound behind her. She looked back and saw Laird looking at Christopher. And Christopher looking at Laird. They both looked at her.

Gwen released a breath of pure unadulterated relief.

"Oh, thank God."

CHAPTER SIXTEEN

Laird and Christopher, blushing and unable to make eye contact, shuffled into Gwen's kitchen in their school uniforms. They'd brought the wedding dress and veil, which they surrendered to her. She draped them over a chair.

"So...true love?" she asked, setting two steaming mugs of hot chocolate in front of them at the kitchen table.

Both laughed nervously.

"I think so," Laird said. "I know you probably think it's gross or wrong or—"

"No, stop right there," Gwen said. "I have no problem at all with two guys being together. Not at all. Not in the least. I'm putting that on the table right now. I'm not judging you for your relationship. I'm judging you for scaring the holy living hell out of me. Now talk."

Christopher shrugged and stirred his hot chocolate.

"I don't know what to say, Miss Ashby," he said. "Laird got here three years ago and it was just...we were friends first. Then best friends. And then Laird admitted he felt something more for me. And I told him I felt the same. And then we started, you know, doing stuff together. I mean, a lot of—"

"You don't have to go into any of the 'doing stuff' details," Gwen said. "I'm a grown-up. I know what two people who love each other do in private together."

"Obviously," Laird said, and Gwen glared at him.

"We're not talking about me tonight," she said.

"Anyway," Laird said. "Miss Muir found out. She was furious. She lectured us on Hell and sin and what an abomination it was."

"How did she find out?" Gwen asked. "Like I did?"

"No," Christopher said. He pointed at Laird with his thumb. "This genius passed me a note in class. She intercepted it."

"Let me guess," Gwen said. "She also showed it to Headmaster Yorke?"

Christopher nodded.

"I thought we'd get kicked out," Laird said. "It was me and Chris and Miss Muir all in the headmaster's office. He took our side against her. She said we had to be expelled, that the sin must be—"

"Rooted out," Gwen finished.

"Yes, exactly," Christopher said. "How did you know?"

"I found a draft of a letter she eventually sent to Edwin. I mean, Headmaster Yorke. That's what the letter said. There was a dangerous evil in the school—sin—and that the sin needed to be rooted out before it spread like a disease."

"Mixed metaphors," Laird said, shaking his head. "An English teacher should have known better."

"She really should have," Gwen agreed. "So what happened? She quit?"

"Headmaster Yorke fired her. Fired her in front of us," Christopher said.

"It was bitchin'," Laird said, smiling hugely. "I mean, it was nice of him. Sorry."

"It's okay. That would have been bitchin'," she said, smiling at his old-fashioned slang. She took a sip of her tea. "I'm very glad he fired her."

"She stormed out. She was so pissed I thought she'd come back and kill us all with a Tommy gun or something. She left that day. Left everything behind," Laird said. "Took one suitcase and was gone. Good riddance."

"But it was scary," Christopher said. "She said she was going to tell my parents. She was going to tell everyone's parents."

Laird stared down into his hot chocolate. He hadn't taken a sip of it. "My parents already know what I am. They knew when I was fourteen. That's why they kicked me out."

"They kicked you out?"

He nodded. "I stayed with an aunt for a while. She was worse than my parents. She thought she could reform me."

"Reform you," Gwen said, already disgusted with where this was headed.

"She hit him," Christopher said. Laird stared into a corner of the kitchen, not making eye contact with either of them. "Tell her what she did, Laird."

"It doesn't matter," Laird said.

"Tell her. She should know." Christopher looked at Gwen, who reached across the table and covered Laird's hand with hers.

Laird glanced at Christopher and nodded. She'd noticed before how the two of them could communicate with glances, like they shared a secret intimate language. Now she knew why.

"Laird's aunt locked him in a room with, you know...a prostitute."

"My aunt paid her to make a man out of me," Laird said.

Christopher shook his head. "He broke a window to get out. Had big scratches on his arm from the glass. Still had them when he got here."

"God, that's awful," Gwen said, tears burning her eyes. She gave Laird's hand a reassuring squeeze.

"That's why we became friends," Christopher continued. "I saw the bandage on his arm. I asked if he was okay."

Gwen's throat tightened. These poor boys. What sort of awful backward world did they come from? Hellfire and brimstone teachers? Hiring a prostitute to "reform" a gay teenage boy? What century were they living in? Thank God Edwin was headmaster here and took care of them like he did. Someone needed to. Everyone else had seemingly turned their backs on them.

"How did you get here?" she asked Laird, hoping to bring him back from whatever dark place he'd gone to in his mind. "At the school, I mean."

"My aunt lives about an hour from here. I heard about

this school from a teacher, and I wrote Headmaster Yorke a letter asking what I had to do to get in and get a scholarship. He wrote back and arranged for me to come here. When I told him my parents kicked me out, he promised this place could be my home."

"That explains why you were in Miss Muir's grade book but not on the address list."

"No address," he said. "I mean, except for this one. Headmaster Yorke saved my life. I think I would have killed myself if I had to stay with my aunt another day."

"I asked the headmaster what was going on with this mysterious Bride person," Gwen said. "He wouldn't tell me anything. And I'll admit, that made me very angry at him for keeping it a secret from me."

"Don't be mad at the headmaster," Laird begged. "It's not his fault. I begged him not to tell anyone about Chris and me. His parents would go bonkers if they found out. And he swore on his honor as a gentleman he would keep our secret to the grave and even after."

Gwen's stomach dropped. She should've known. She should've guessed Edwin, upright and honorable to a fault, had a good reason for keeping her in the dark about the true identity of the Bride.

"I'm sure he wanted to tell you," Christopher said. "We wanted to tell you, but we just didn't know if we could, you know—"

"Trust me?" Gwen asked.

The boys nodded.

"You can trust me, I promise," she said. "And just to be clear...there never was a Bride, was there? This was all a prank, you said."

"We're in separate dorms," Laird explained. "I needed an excuse to sneak out. We spread rumors of a ghost haunting campus. Eventually, we let a few of the younger boys see me in the dress from a safe distance. From then on, I wore it when going out after dark. If anyone caught us, they would think we were just out trying to prank them into believing the Bride was real."

"And the dress belonged to Miss Muir," Christopher said with a wicked grin. "Kind of fun to desecrate it."

"Have you thought about telling the other boys?" she asked. "These are your schoolmates and friends. They might surprise you."

"It would break their hearts to find out the Bride wasn't real," Laird said with a grin.

Gwen glared at him. He knew exactly what she was asking about.

"We've talked about it," Christopher quickly said. "They might accept it. They might accept *us*. Maybe. But they'd look at us differently. I don't want that."

"Me neither," Laird said. "It's an all-boys school. I don't want anybody to think I'm, you know…"

"Attracted to them?" Gwen asked.

"Right," Laird said. "It's just Chris. I mean, Headmaster Yorke isn't bad, but he's too old for me."

"And he's taken," Gwen said, swatting his hand.

After they finished their tea, she gave both boys big hugs and ordered Laird to retire the Bride charade to avoid giving her—or any of the other teachers—heart trouble. She didn't even have to mention how inappropriate it was that he'd been sneaking in and out of her private residence for the dress. He promised on his honor as a Marshal boy that the Bride had taken her last stroll across campus. How Laird and Christopher would meet without the ruse was a discussion for later, a discussion that would involve the headmaster. This was clearly above Gwen's pay grade.

She sent them off to bed. If anyone asked where they'd been, Laird and Christopher could tell them they were helping Miss Ashby with some heavy lifting. She'd back them up.

One terrifying mystery solved. A weight off Gwen's shoulders.

That only left the question of her car. What the hell had happened to it? She could only begin to guess. It simply didn't seem possible she'd walked away from the wreck with only the minor injuries she'd sustained—all long healed—if the car had been totaled like that.

Well, she'd worry about it tomorrow. Tonight she was so relieved she'd figured out the mystery of the Bride and the secret of Miss Muir she could have cried.

And she did cry. Edwin was no villain. He'd promised the boys to keep their relationship a secret to the grave and he'd kept his promise. He was an honorable fool, and she adored him for it.

She'd go to him tomorrow and apologize. She'd go and tell him that she should have trusted him and would trust him from now on. And she'd tell him he was a hero to her for standing up for Laird and Christopher and not judging or condemning them the way Miss Muir had. She admired him for being so noble he would sacrifice his own heart to keep a promise to two scared teenage boys in love. And she would tell him she loved him. She knew it was crazy to love him so much so quickly. But she'd never done anything crazy in her life until asking for directions to the school in that diner. That one crazy thing was the best decision she'd ever made, because it had led her straight to Edwin.

"Why am I not telling him all of this to his face?" she asked herself out loud.

She couldn't come up with a single good answer for that. After straightening her hair and clothes, she raced across campus, keeping an eye out for that damn snake again. But not even snakes or lions or tigers or bears—or boys in wedding dresses—would keep her from Edwin tonight.

She knocked on the headmaster's door, and he opened it only moments later. As late as it was, she had expected him to be in a robe and slippers. Instead, he was —again—fully dressed in his suit minus only his jacket. Did he sleep like this? No problem. Only a bit more work for her when she started ripping his clothes off.

"I met the Bride," she said.

"So you're here to apologize, I presume?" he asked, a smug smile on his face.

"No, I'm not."

"Then why, pray tell, are you here, Miss Ashby?"

"To tell you I love you."

CHAPTER SEVENTEEN

Edwin took a deep breath. "Are you quite certain of that?" he asked, crossing his arms over his chest.

"I am absolutely certain of it," Gwen said. "And I'll be the first to admit how crazy that sounds. I've been here for two weeks. But in two weeks I've fallen in love. And not just with you, but with this school. The grounds, the buildings, the boys."

"You're in love with the boys? All of them or—"

"Oh, not that way and you know it," she said, laughing. "Christopher and Laird were in one of the turrets tonight. No secret what they were doing there. I talked to them for a long time. They told me how..." Gwen broke off mid-sentence. "Can I come inside and have this conversation with you? Or are you going to make me stand out here in the hallway?"

"Will you behave if I let you in?" Edwin asked, giving her a suspicious look.

"No."

"Then you may come in." He stepped aside and ushered her through the door. She was pleased when he shut and locked it behind him. Good. She didn't want to leave ever again anyway.

They sat side by side on the leather sofa.

"So Laird and Christopher told me what happened with Miss Muir, how she found a note Laird wrote to Christopher."

Edwin's eyes went comically wide. "Not just any note."

"Passionate little missive, was it?"

"*Explicit* would be the better word for it. I'm not sure I've recovered yet from reading it."

Gwen laughed. "Teenage boys. All hormones, very little brains."

"You aren't bothered by their relationship?"

"Of course not," Gwen said. "Don't be silly. It's not the nineteenth century. And it's not like we have to worry about teen pregnancy in this situation."

"One blessing," Edwin said.

"They said you fired Miss Muir right in front of them."

Edwin clasped his hands between his knees. "I realize that was inappropriate," he said, sounding remorseful. "But her accusations infuriated me. They're boys in love, not Nazis or demons. And there's precedent for it. Ancient Greek soldiers—"

"Edwin."

"Yes, back on the topic. Miss Muir acted like Satan himself had come to this school. It was fundamentalist lunacy. And the boys didn't deserve to hear any of that hateful nonsense. I sent Miss Muir packing immediately."

"You never told the school she was fired?"

Edwin shook his head and leaned back. "I couldn't. That would have raised many questions among the students and staff. I promised the boys I'd guard their secret to the grave and beyond. I said Miss Muir had left to get married. Which was not entirely untrue. She was engaged to a man from her church. No one questioned the explanation."

"And then I turned up."

"And that is something for which I am deeply grateful." Edwin looked at her and smiled. "I wanted to tell you the truth, Gwendolyn. I simply couldn't. I hope you understand why."

"I do, you annoyingly honorable man."

"And you forgive me?"

"Of course not," she said. "I mean, you did the right thing. It's my fault I didn't trust you. Although in fairness, you were being rather cagey."

"I did want to tell you."

"I promise, I'll trust you from now on. Do you forgive me?"

"No," he said, laying his hand on her knee. "Nothing to forgive. You did the right thing. In your shoes, I would have been equally suspicious and concerned for the welfare of the students."

"So we were both right. That never happens. This place really is magical," she said, smiling around the room.

Edwin touched her face. "It's certainly felt like that ever since you came here."

She took his glasses off and sat them on the table.

"Shall we go make some magic in your bedroom?" she asked, the heat of his hand sinking into her skin and permeating her entire body.

Edwin sighed and pulled his hand from her face.

"What is it? Edwin?" Gwen prompted, suddenly scared.

"As much as I would love to, and I promise you, Gwendolyn, I would love to...I feel like our continued relationship would set a bad example for the school. Thanks to your...enthusiasm last Friday, they know we're lovers. I don't know how I can teach them to be gentlemen if I'm having a dalliance with one of the teachers without even an engagement or understanding between us."

Gwen's stomach dropped. "So you're saying we have to stop seeing each other because of your overdeveloped sense of duty and chivalry?"

"No," he said, moving from the couch to the floor. Kneeling in front of her he took her hand in his and brought it to his lips. "I'm saying that I would like to request the honor of your hand in marriage."

"Oh my God," Gwen said, her eyes widening, her stomach flipping backward over itself. "You're serious?"

"I have never been so serious in my life. I have never loved anyone before. Never been loved. And you came here and now here I am, loved and loving. I pray this never ends. When a man sees something good in the world, he should honor it, cherish it, and protect it. I look at you and I see something good and beautiful. Let me honor you and cherish you and protect you. And love you. For always. Will you say yes?"

Gwen stared at him, overwhelmed with joy and fear

and shock and desire. She was speechless, voiceless, thoughtless. It took everything in her power to summon the strength to even say a single word to Edwin at that moment. But she did, and it was the right word.

"Yes."

Although she knew it was crazy to get engaged to someone after knowing him for two weeks, she knew *yes* was the right answer, the only answer, and she had no other answer. She belonged here, belonged to this school, and belonged with Edwin forever.

He pulled a ring from his pocket, a delicate band topped with a gleaming white pearl. He slipped it on her finger, and it fit her as if it had been molded for her hand from magic.

She took Edwin's too-handsome face in her hands and kissed him like she'd die if she didn't. And he kissed her back again and again.

"Now can we go to your bedroom?" she asked.

"You don't even have to ask." Edwin stood up, pulled her into his arms, and kissed her all the way to the door to his bedroom. She reached for the doorknob. "Wait."

"Wait?" Gwen asked.

"You didn't say *yes* to my proposal just so I would make love to you, did you?"

"No, of course not." She grinned at him. "Not entirely, anyway."

Edwin threw the door open and carried her to the bed. She sat on the side, and Edwin stood in front of her. With his face in her hands, he bent and kissed her again, as if it had been an eon between the last time she'd been in his bedroom and not mere days. It felt like an eon.

She'd never let another night pass without sharing a bed with Edwin. Not if she could help it.

He brusquely unbuttoned her blouse and soon it ended up on the floor. She took off her bra and tossed it aside. He laid her on her back and slid off her skirt and panties. Soon she lay completely naked across the made bed. He crawled to her and knelt between her open legs.

She watched him remove his vest and shirt. Why didn't every man on earth wear three-piece suits? Because the women of the world would never be able to think straight, that was why. She'd have to bar Edwin from her classroom so she could concentrate on her lessons without imagining biting those buttons off his vest and kissing every square inch of his broad, muscular chest with the perfect amount of chest hair.

He undid his tie last and gazed at her body with reverent desire and unrepentant hunger. He held her breasts in his hands, and she arched underneath him, offering herself up to him. He massaged her breasts and nipples. Teased them. Kneaded them. Soon she was panting, almost to the point of begging.

"Please, Edwin..."

"Let me enjoy you," he said. "I want to take my time with my future wife."

She smiled up at him. How could she argue with that? It was their first time together as an engaged couple. She could sense the specialness of the moment. No, they shouldn't rush it. She wanted to cherish the memory of this night forever.

He ran his hands up and down the front of her body from her hips to her chest and back again. He caressed all her curves—her thighs, her hips, her small waist, her full breasts, her shoulders. She ached to have his hard length filling her, but she bit her tongue to stop her pleas. He would have her when he wanted her. No sooner.

With a hand on either side of her head, he dipped his mouth to hers and kissed her lightly, his lips taunting hers. She rose up to deepen the kiss, but he pulled back. Groaning, she lay back again, and he laughed at her.

"Be a good girl," he said.

"You always have to be in charge, don't you?" she asked.

"I'm the headmaster. I *am* in charge."

He proved then how truly he was in charge by pressing a deep and possessive kiss onto her mouth. His tongue explored her lips. She couldn't get enough of the taste of him—a touch of wine, a touch of tea—and the warm manly scent of him, like cedar soap and honorable intentions.

She raised her hands to his shoulders, needing to feel the heat of his body. His muscles tensed under her touch. Every inch of him was granite-hard. He kissed a trail from her lips to her nipples. He rolled his tongue around them, sucked them, teased them. Ripples of excitement coursed through her breasts, through her body, sending her inner muscles twitching and tightening with desire.

"You make me feel so beautiful," she said as Edwin slid his hands up and down her inner thighs.

"You are beautiful. I've never seen a woman so beautiful. Here," he said, caressing her face with the back of his hand. "And here." He ran his hand over her shoulders and breasts. "And here," he said, cupping her heat with his hand and slipping two fingers into her wetness.

She gasped at the sudden penetration. She needed this, needed him inside her. Her muscles tightened around him as he explored inside her. Whenever her breathing changed, he stopped and gave that part of her extra attention. She felt so open, so ready to be filled up with him, by him.

"Edwin, please," she begged again. "I need you in me."

He laughed softly. "Far be it from me to deny a lady such a humble request."

He opened his pants and pulled himself free. She watched with ever-increasing desire as he stroked himself. She loved seeing him touch himself. She loved seeing her touching him even more. She reached between her thighs and took him in her hand, guiding him into her. With torturous slowness, he sank inch by inch into her body. She enveloped him with her heat, raising her hips to take him as deep as she could. He filled her perfectly, stretching her wet walls open as she shivered from the unbearable pleasure of him penetrating her to the very core.

"Edwin..." She heaved a ragged breath as he moved in her. He pulled out to the tip before pushing back in with a hard, deliberate thrust. His movements were measured, which only added to the intensity. She wanted him to lose himself in her, to lose control. But he held himself solid and still over her, only his hips moving as he set the pace and made her wait for it.

Two could play at that game. She ran her hands over his arms and chest, kissed his collarbone, nibbled his neck. She wrapped her legs around his back and whispered her love and lust for him and all the things she dreamed they would do someday in this bed. He thrust harder and faster. He cupped the back of her head and brought her neck to his mouth. He devoured her throat with kisses that left her moaning with need. Her hips pumped against his. She wanted to come, needed to come—

With her eyes shut tight and her fingers digging into his shoulders, she came. The orgasm racked her body, and once it had passed, she collapsed under him. At last, Edwin let go of what little remained of his self-control, riding her with quick desperate thrusts before he came inside her, shivering in her arms.

Edwin pulled out of her and lay on his side, flush against her. He draped his arm over her stomach.

"Good Lord," he said.

"My sentiments exactly." Gwen giggled girlishly. "It will always be like this, won't it? You and I?"

"Yes," he said, his voice strangely somber. "Nothing will change. Nothing at all."

She smiled up at the scarlet canopy. "Good," she said, and laughed again, this time louder.

"What is so funny, Miss Ashby?" Edwin demanded.

"I'm engaged to be married to a man I've known for two weeks who is headmaster at the school where I work. An all-boys boarding school in the middle of nowhere with no internet, no cell phone service, and no computers." She sighed. "Edwin, I used to be so sensible."

"What happened?"

"I came to my senses."

CHAPTER EIGHTEEN

Gwen awoke at dawn in a small panic that her time at Marshal had all been a dream. A wonderful magical mid-autumn's night dream. If Edwin, still asleep beside her, wasn't real enough to dispel that notion, the ring on her finger was. She raised her left hand and stared at it in the pale morning light filtering through the stained-glass window.

Had she dreamed up her own engagement ring it would have been this one. Silver and pearl. So simple, so elegant. And not a diamond in sight. She'd read once about the children who were forced to work diamond mines in Africa like slaves. No diamonds for her. How had Edwin known this was her dream ring?

Because he was Edwin and he knew her. And because he knew her, he knew she would sneak out and go back to her cottage to get ready for class. She kissed his sleeping lips and dragged herself from his bed. It was easy to leave this morning because she knew she would return to his bed tonight and every night hereafter. She dressed quietly and slipped out into a perfect September sunrise.

A sense of peace consumed Gwen. Everything was perfect. Almost too perfect. She knew she shouldn't question the good gifts that the world graciously bestowed, but enough of the sensible old Gwen remained to make her wonder why everything was so...completely...perfect...

Gwen paused mid-step. In the middle of campus, a woman stood silent in the early morning mist. An old woman with white hair and a face lined with a lifetime of penance.

"Ma'am?" Gwen called out as she neared the woman. The woman didn't seem to hear her.

She called out again. Once more the old woman did nothing but gaze upon the campus surrounding her. She looked at it and through it at the same time.

"Grandma? Where did you go?" A young man's voice came from the entrance to the courtyard. He jogged over to the old woman but didn't give Gwen, only a stone's throw from her, so much as a glance.

"I'm here, Ryan," the old woman said.

"You wandered off. Scared me to death." Ryan looked only about twenty or so, not much older than Gwen's oldest students.

"Death?" the old woman said with a sad smile on her face. "You're just a child, Ryan. What do you know about death?"

"Grandma, let's go. You saw the school. We should leave."

She shook her head. Gwen waved her hand in front of

the old woman. She didn't even blink and neither did her grandson. They acted like she was invisible. What was going on?

"This is no school," the old woman said. "This is a tomb."

Gwen shivered at the word *tomb*. Who was this mad woman?

"You know what I mean," the young man, Ryan, said. "It was a school. You've seen it. Let's go."

"I was a teacher here," the old woman said. "Long ago."

"I know," Ryan said. "You told me that."

"I told you nothing," she said.

Gwen narrowed her eyes at the woman. "Miss Muir?"

"I taught literature here," she said to her son, again ignoring Gwen. "From 1961 until 1964. I remember it was 1964. That's when we saw *Mary Poppins.*"

"1964?" Gwen repeated to herself.

"Gwendolyn?"

Gwen turned around and saw Edwin standing ten feet away from her in his three-piece suit.

"Edwin, what's happening?" she asked, more scared now than she'd ever been of the Bride.

"I wanted to tell you," he said and gave her a look of profound apology. "But how could I?"

"Let me tell you about death," the old woman said. Gwen turned from Edwin back to her. "I was an educated woman. But I was a fool. I loved this place. Loved this school. The headmaster here was a kind and noble man. Edwin Yorke. We all called him Headmaster Yorke out of respect."

"I'm sure he respected you, too, Grandma."

"He did once. But then I lost his respect. There were two boys at the school. The boys...they loved each other. I found out they loved each other. I..." The old woman raised a bony hand to her mouth. "I told the headmaster what I learned. I thought it was a sin. The gravest of sins."

"It was 1964," Ryan said. "Everyone thought it was a sin back then."

"Not Headmaster Yorke. I thought he would throw them out, but instead he fired me. He was right to do it."

"I'm sure he forgave you."

Gwen listened in growing horror. 1964, Ryan said? No...it couldn't be. No. No. Was she having a nightmare?

"I wrote letters to the parents about the school, about what Headmaster Yorke was allowing to happen on his watch. Boys engaging in sinful acts with the other boys. I told them to take their children out of the school if they cared at all for their souls."

"Grandma..." Ryan sounded horrified. Gwen shared his shock.

"They came, the parents did. Christopher's parents came first, I heard. They came at night a few days after I sent the first letter. They came and grabbed Christopher from his bed and tried to drag him from the school to their car. He fought them off. In the struggle..."

The old woman covered her face with both hands. She took a deep shattered breath.

"In the struggle, someone knocked over an oil lamp. The rug caught fire and spread quickly to the curtains. Soon the dormitory was in blazes. The boys were sound asleep. But they woke up and ran for their lives."

"That's good then, right?" Ryan asked.

The old woman shook her head.

Gwen looked back over her shoulder. Edwin no longer stood alone on the lawn in the rising sun. Every last student now flanked him—Edwin in the middle, fifteen boys on each side.

"A boy named Samuel got trapped inside the school," the old woman continued. "Headmaster Yorke raced in to rescue him. Christopher and Laird followed him into the fire. Then...part of the roof collapsed. And the fire spread to the other dorm—Pembroke. Every single last student ran back into the burning buildings trying to save their headmaster and the other students."

Gwen held her hands to her face and looked from the aged woman to Edwin, who stood silent and solemn in the morning light. The boys stared at the woman. They saw her. She did not see them.

"Headmaster Yorke had taught them far too well the lessons of loyalty and brotherhood. That was the motto of the school, Ryan. A Latin motto."

"*Fortius quam fraternitas nullum est vinculum*," Edwin said, his voice crisp and commanding as a ship's captain.

"There is no bond stronger than brotherhood," the boys said in unison.

The old woman didn't hear them, but recited the English phrase softly to herself.

"And then the roof collapsed completely. And Headmaster Yorke and all the boys were trapped inside."

"Oh my God," Ryan said, his hand on his stomach as if he was about to be ill.

"They all died," the woman said. "Died together."

*"There is no bond stronger than brotherhood," the boys
said in unison.*

"*Fidus ultra finem,*" Edwin said.

"Faithful beyond the end," all the boys replied.

"Fifty years ago today..." The old woman looked at her grandson. "They all died...every last one of them. Here on campus. Two of the teachers, Mr. Price and Mr. Reynolds, died of smoke inhalation. But the rest of the boys burned to death, burned beyond recognition. They could only identify two. One was Samuel. Headmaster Yorke had shielded him from the fire as best he could. And they identified Christopher. We think it was Laird who covered his body to protect him from the fire. Thirty-three dead in total. All because of me."

"Grandma, there was no way you could have seen this would happen."

"No. But it's done and those beautiful boys and their headmaster and teachers are all dead. Headmaster Yorke would have been ninety years old this year had he lived. My age."

"Come on, Grandma," Ryan said, gently taking her by the arm. "We should go."

"They're all buried here, you know." She pointed across the campus. Gwen followed her finger and saw that all the Marshal buildings were gone now. Only an empty field greeted her. An empty field and thirty-three graves in the ground. She didn't have to get close to them to know that, although their birth years differed, every last one was inscribed with the same death year: 1964.

"The parents buried their sons together. They died together trying to save each other. They would be buried together. Together for eternity."

A tear spilled out of Ryan's eye and rolled down his cheek.

"I want to be buried here, too," Miss Muir said.

"Grandma, don't talk like that."

The old woman shook her head. "But I don't deserve to be buried here. For fifty years, I have prayed for forgiveness. I asked God to somehow take back what I'd done. I'd half believed that if you brought me here, I'd see the buildings standing again. Hawkwood Hall— that's where I taught my classes. The headmaster lived on the fifth floor. And there was a cottage right over there." She pointed at Gwen's house. "I lived there. And you see those patches where there's no grass? That's where the two dorms were...Pembroke and Newbury... side by side."

Gwen sobbed in silence, afraid to miss any word the old woman spoke.

"I prayed God would bring the school back, and the boys, and Headmaster Yorke. And they would be together. These boys...this school was their Heaven. And I prayed they would have a teacher come take my place who would not make the mistakes I made, not be the fool I was. And she would love and cherish the boys and Headmaster Yorke. That is what I have prayed for."

"I'm sure they're all in Heaven," Ryan said and touched his grandmother's arm.

"But I won't be," the old woman said. "I'll go to Hell for what I've done. I will burn as they burned. Except my burning will never end."

Gwen inhaled deeply and smelled the smoke again. It came not from the burned rubble of the buildings or the scorched grass, or even from the past. It came from the old woman, from Miss Muir.

"Forgive me, Edwin," the old woman said. "Forgive me."

"I forgive you," Edwin said. But the old woman didn't hear him. "We all forgive you."

"Take me home," the old woman instructed her grandson. "I was wrong to come here. I don't belong here. I never did."

Ryan took his grandmother by the arm and began to lead her away. Gwen took a step, intending to follow her.

"Gwendolyn, you can leave," Edwin called out. She turned and faced him. "You can leave, but if you do leave, there's no coming back."

"And if I stay?" she asked.

"Then you will stay here always. Just as we have, just as we are."

Last night she had lain next to him in his bed and asked him to promise her that nothing would ever change, that it would always be this wonderful, this passionate, this good. A foolish romantic question, the sort of question everyone asks when they first fall in love. The answer should have been *no*. Of course it wouldn't always be like this. They would grow older, grow wiser, and grow more comfortable with each other. The passion would wax and wane. And then someday it would end. It would all end, because no one lives forever.

But Edwin was already dead.

He'd been dead for decades.

"It's so strange," the old woman whispered as her grandson escorted her to their car. "I had such a vivid dream last night. I dreamed that I came back here and the school was still here and it looked like it did fifty years ago. The boys were all here—Christopher and Laird, Jefferson, Samuel, Eliot...all my sweet young gentlemen. And Headmaster Yorke was here. And a lady. They'd decorated the whole school in white for a wedding. I thought it was my wedding. But it wasn't. I wasn't even a guest at the wedding. They didn't want me here..."

Ryan tried to coax her toward the exit. "We'll go now, Grandma. You have to eat, take your medicine."

"They rebuilt the school, Ryan. But it wasn't my Marshal. Five miles from here is the new school. The Marshal School, they call it. It's not the same, though. It's not the same at all...."

The old woman and her grandson walked back through the arch.

Gwen brought a hand to her face and found it wet with tears. She looked back and saw the crosses were gone now, all those graves, replaced with the campus as she had known it. The boys were still in a line, Edwin in their midst.

"There was no way to tell you," Edwin said. "Forgive me."

She raised her hand to stop his words.

It all made sense now. The waitress at the diner...it was the Marshal *School*, the new school, that was hiring teachers, not the Marshal *Academy*. And when the waitress had given the old man extra napkins...she knew he would cry like Christopher's grandfather had when he'd visited.

No. Not his grandfather. It had been his father come

to mourn the fiftieth anniversary of the school burning to the ground, the anniversary of the day he'd killed his son by trying to save him from his "sins."

No computers or cell phones. The shock over Edwin's divorce. "The war"—not the Gulf War, but World War II.

And, of course, the scent of smoke.

Now that the old woman—Miss Muir—had gone, the scent of smoke disappeared from Gwen's nostrils, and all she could smell was the dewy grass beneath her feet, the warm and living forest. Life. She smelled life. Even though all her boys...

"My sweet boys," she said and looked at their faces, eternally frozen in youth. Somehow Miss Muir's prayer had been answered. The school lived. The boys lived. The headmaster lived. "My angels..."

All of them dead fifty years, and yet here they were and here they would stay. Miss Muir's wish had been granted—the school had risen from the ashes, the boys from their graves. Here was the school, the boys, the headmaster...and Miss Muir couldn't even see it and never would. Her prayer had been answered and she would never know it. Their Heaven was her Hell.

But what about Gwen?

She looked to the parking lot, where Ryan was helping his grandmother into their car. Not far away sat the wreckage of Gwen's car. The battered, fiery wreckage...

"Gwendolyn?" She heard the voice calling her name. Not Edwin's voice. Not the boys'. She'd never heard the voice before. Her eyelids fluttered. She blinked and blinked again. A white light flashed. She closed her eyes tight and opened them again. She lay in a hospital bed, and above her stood a man in a doctor's scrubs and coat.

"Gwendolyn Ashby. Can you hear me?" asked the doctor. "You're in the hospital. You were in a car accident, and you've been unconscious. Nod if you understand."

Gwen closed her eyes again. When she opened them, she was back at Marshal, back with Edwin.

"Edwin?" she said, her voice trembling with fear and confusion.

"You can go back if you wish," Edwin said to Gwen. "Or you can stay and…"

He didn't have to finish his sentence. If she stayed it would be like he promised—always like this. The days would blur into each other in a haze of books and laughter and learning. The nights would be like last night always. Heated, ardent, hungry. Every night like the first night. New love forever.

The old world was there, waiting for her. She could wake up and rejoin it. But if she left, she could not return. If she stayed, she would never leave. The door that had let her in would close for good. Somehow she knew she would forget this morning and Miss Muir's visit like one forgot a dream upon waking. The boys would forget. Edwin would forget. This would be her life forever and her life would be…

"Perfect," she whispered.

She walked up to Edwin. Thirty pairs of eyes watched her.

"Boys," she said. "Don't look."

The boys covered their eyes with both hands.

She put her hand on the back of Edwin's neck and pulled his mouth down to hers for a long hard kiss.

Thirty boys *ohhh*-ed and wolf-whistled before bursting into embarrassed teenage laughter. Behind them, the bell broke through the morning fog and sounded the five-minute warning to get to first period.

"Boys," Edwin said sternly as he raised his head from the kiss. "Class. Now."

The boys, all of them wearing watchful smiles, didn't move a muscle.

Silly boys. Didn't they know they were starting *A Midsummer Night's Dream* in class today? Surely they were eager for that discussion.

She gave Edwin one more kiss and headed toward Hawkwood Hall.

"You heard the headmaster," Gwen said and clapped her hands once to get their attention. "Get to class."

Somewhere in the back of her mind, she heard the sound of a heart rate monitor flat-lining.

Gwen ignored it and went back to work.

ABOUT THE AUTHOR

Tiffany Reisz is the *USA Today* bestselling author of the Romance Writers of America RITA®-winning Original Sinners series from Harlequin's Mira Books.

Her erotic fantasy *The Red*—the first entry in the Godwicks series, self-published under the banner 8th Circle Press—was named an NPR Best Book of the Year and a Goodreads Best Romance of the Month.

Tiffany lives in Kentucky with her husband and two cats. The cats are not writers.

www.tiffanyreisz.com

ABOUT THE ILLUSTRATOR

Andrew Shaffer is the *New York Times* bestselling author and illustrator of the children's books *Mothman's Merry Cryptid Christmas* and the sequel, *Mothman's Happy Cryptid Halloween.*

He is a five-time Goodreads Choice Award nominee and a two-time finalist in the Humor category. His award-winning illustrations have appeared in *Heavy Metal* magazine, Comedy Central's *The Colbert Report,* and on book covers worldwide.

Andrew lives in Kentucky with his wife and two cats. The cats are not artists.

www.andrewshaffer.com